THE ADVENTURES OF
MALI & KEELA

A VIRTUES BOOK FOR CHILDREN

By
JONATHAN COLLINS

WITH JANICE HEALEY, ILLUSTRATED BY JENNY COOPER

BOOKS FOR ALL THAT YOU ARE

PERSONHOOD PRESS

THE ADVENTURES OF MALI & KEELA:
A VIRTUES BOOK FOR CHILDREN

Copyright © 2010 by Jonathan Collins

For permission or book ordering information contact the publisher:

Personhood Press
PO Box 370
Fawnskin, CA 92333
(800) 429-1192
Fax: (909) 866-2961
www.personhoodpress.com
info@personhoodpress.com

Library of Congress Control Number: 2009938261

ISBN: 9781932181524

This book was printed in April 2010 at
Friesens Book Division, Altona, Manitoba R0G 0B0, Canada

Cover Design: Jonathan Collins
Interior Design: Jonathan Collins
Edited by: Sean O'Connor
Illustrations: Jenny Cooper

Source Note:

Virtues definitions are used with permission from Virtues Project International www.virtuesproject.com

Virtues definitions are adapted from The Virtues Project Educator's Guide: Simple Ways to Create a Culture of Character *(pp. 135-237), by L. K. Povov, 2000, Austin, TX: PRO-ED. Copyright 2000 by Linda Kavelin-Popov. Adapted with permission.*

For Jemma, Liam, and Natalie.

CONTENTS

Foreword

When we founded The Virtues Project in 1991, my brother John Kavelin, my husband Dr. Dan Popov, and I had a dream that we could make a difference in the world. When we self-published our first book, *The Family Virtues Guide*, we hoped to inspire both children and adults to awaken to their full potential, emotionally, intellectually and spiritually. Our vision was to help children discover who they truly are – people of kindness, creativity, excellence, and integrity.

The world needs people willing to take personal responsibility, to live by a strong sense of purpose, to serve and enrich the world.

We have been amazed by the rapid and sustained spread of The Virtues Project as a global grass roots movement. It is now in more than 95 countries, helping individuals to live more authentic and meaningful lives, parents to raise respectful, optimistic children, and schools to create a culture of caring and character. Communities and even countries are finding the Five Virtues Strategies a way to transform violence to virtues.

There is now a new wellspring of creativity illuminating the virtues valued by all cultures. *The Adventures of Mali and Keela* is a beautiful example, one we heartily recommend to all parents seeking tools for bringing out the best in their children, and of course, themselves.

These delightful and imaginative stories, and simple exercises, give you a way to spend loving time with your children while encouraging them to reflect on, and practice, their virtues. Character is destiny, and virtues are the content of our character - our greatest treasure.

This little book encourages us, as Ghandi said, to "be the change you wish to see in the world."

With enthusiasm and gratitude,
Linda Kavelin Popov
Co-founder of The Virtues Project

Preface

When our children were young, my wife and I attended a Virtues Project™ (see p. 143) weekend which had a profound impact on how we parented. Concepts such as 'speaking the language of the virtues' and 'recognizing teachable moments' sat beautifully with our personal ideas about parenting and teaching. Natalie, a trained Montessori teacher, saw The Virtues Project™ as a valuable complement to her work in the classroom.

At the same time, our then five-year-old son was putting me on the spot each evening – I'd begun a tradition of making up 'Mali stories' at bedtime... and these improvised tales of adventure and daring were expected each night. Mali (an anagram of his name, Liam) was a swashbuckling hero who displayed the virtues – courage, joyfulness, determination, etc. – that both he and I loved hearing about.

And then the penny dropped for me... I realized these stories were a fantastic way to help understand virtues. While the characters sailed the seas and saved the day, they educated and inspired. I started writing down the stories with the intention of creating this book.

The Virtues Project™ brings virtues into everyday life. Some of the virtues are reasonably easy for young children to understand – caring, friendliness, enthusiasm, etc. – but some are a little more difficult. Humility, tact, respect, integrity, and so on, are reasonably complex for a young mind to grasp. When they are demonstrated through the actions of our heroes, the message is so much easier to communicate, and the understanding is easier to absorb.

As with the original Mali stories, the intention for this book is that the adult reads the story to the child. Discussion pages follow each story, containing definitions (from *The Virtues Project™ Educator's Guide*) of the virtues shown in the story, followed by questions, written as a prompt for discussion.

To ensure the stories are engaging for the child, the examples of virtues within them have been consciously kept light. As with the fables of old, the yarn drives the interest, allowing the virtue to be communicated subtly. The stories touch on the virtue, with the following discussion pages picking up from that cue, and taking the exploration further.

The questions provided are examples designed to encourage discussion and interaction. They're a catalyst to stimulate the flow of ideas, and I encourage you to add your own questions to see where the discussion takes you. It is my hope that through this process, a deeper understanding of the virtues will occur for the child.

These stories flow best when read in story order, however, with 'recognizing teachable moments' in mind, they have been written to work also as standalone stories. You may recognize a particular time when it would be helpful to discuss a certain virtue (patience, or tolerance perhaps) with your children, in which case the story specific to that virtue might be a good choice.

While *The Adventures of Mali & Keela* has tapped into the wisdom generously offered by the creators of The Virtues Project™, it is an independent publication. The fifty-two virtues discussed in this book are from *The Virtues Project™ Educator's Guide*, which was designed primarily for counselors, teachers, caregivers, and youth leaders as a guide to creating cultures of caring and integrity in schools, day care centers, and youth programs. These virtues were chosen because of their universality. They may fit very well alongside spiritual belief systems, however they are not specific to any one faith.

Jonathan Collins

THREE MOUNTAIN ISLAND

Determination ⌁ Consideration ⌁ Peacefulness ⌁ Tact

I feel adventure in my bones! Mali thought as he jumped out of bed.

From the window of his tree house he could see over the water to the castle, sparkling in the morning light. It was there that his friend Princess Keela lived.

He climbed down the ladder, prepared his boat, and was soon sailing towards the mainland.

Looking back at his island, Mali smiled. His tree-house looked good up there in the big tree overlooking the bay.

At the castle Mali and Keela planned their adventure.

"There's an island, not too far from here," Mali said, "with three mountains on it. And," he added, "they've never been climbed!"

"Then let's be the first to climb them!" Keela said with a grin.

They told the king and queen their plans, and set sail for Three Mountain Island. It wasn't long before they were standing on the beach looking up at the first mountain.

"It doesn't look too big," Keela said. "Let's go!"

Rough plants scratched their legs as they pushed through the undergrowth. The slope grew steep and thick with trees as they clambered upwards. When they finally stepped out from the trees into the bright sunlight at the top, they realized how high they had climbed.

"Woo hoo!" Keela cried out. "Look at your boat!"

"It looks like a toy down there," Mali laughed.

They rested a while before Keela pointed towards the second mountain. "Let's keep going," she said.

Rocks slid and tumbled as they scrambled upwards. It was hot work but eventually they made it over the ridge. When they saw the view in front of them, their tiredness was quickly forgotten.

A clear blue lake, shimmering in the sun, was nestled between the second mountain and an even bigger one beyond.

"I'll race you to the lake," said Keela, and she was off before Mali could answer.

Mali caught up as they reached the water's edge. A company of emerald-green parrots flew low over the lake. A waterfall splashed on the far side, and the air chimed with birdcalls.

"A perfect spot for a picnic," Mali said as he pulled a bundle of food from his bag. They ate hungrily. They skimmed stones and splashed in the cool water, and then they continued around to the base of the third mountain.

Beside the waterfall they clambered up boulders. Higher and higher they climbed. The stream that fed the waterfall tumbled down the rocks beside them.

"Oh no!" Mali cried as the strap on his shoe broke.

Keela turned to see the shoe tumbling down. It bounced off the rocks and landed with a *splash* in the stream. Then, like a tiny boat, it floated to the edge of the waterfall and disappeared from view.

"Wait here. I'll go and hunt for it," Mali told Keela. "I'll be back soon."

He scrambled down. The rocks were sharp against his bare foot. At the bottom he searched for the shoe – scanning the lake and checking between rocks – but there was no sign of it.

Mali selected a large leaf from a plant that grew beside the lake and wrapped it around his bare foot. Then, with a long flax leaf, he continued to wrap and strap until he had made a leafy shoe.

Then he climbed back up to where Keela waited.

"I'm tuckered," he puffed. He flopped to the ground. His legs ached and his foot hurt. "I don't think I can climb another step."

Far in the distance they could see Mali's boat – so much smaller than when they'd seen it from the first mountain. They looked down at the parrots flying formations around the lake. They talked about how high they'd climbed – and as they talked their determination to reach the top grew.

Mali got to his feet.

"What are you waiting for?" he said. "Let's get going."

"I thought you couldn't climb another step?" said Keela. She looked at Mali's makeshift shoe. "I don't mind if you'd rather we go back down."

"I'm determined to get to the top – I know we can do it!" he replied. "Come on!"

At the first big rock Mali held his hands together to make a step for Keela to put her foot into. He hoisted her up. She then

reached back down to help pull him up. They climbed the last of the rocks this way until eventually they reached the top.

"Wow!" they said together.

Everywhere, as far as they could see, was blue. The blue from the ocean melted into the blue from the sky – it seemed as if they had stepped into a huge blue painting. The only thing not blue was a fountain of white water far below. Beneath the fountain was a grey shape.

"What's that?" Keela whispered. It seemed too amazing to speak aloud.

"I think it's a whale," Mali whispered back. He had never seen one from up above like this. "It's spraying water from its blowhole!"

Mali and Keela sat at the top of the mountain and watched the whale swim gracefully by. They were silent in their blue-painted world.

Gradually their blue world turned indigo.

"We'd better head back down," Mali said.

Beside the lake Keela spotted something nudging the sandy bank.

"Mali!" she called, as she picked up a soggy shoe.

The trek down to the boat went quickly and they were soon ready to set sail.

"We did it!" Mali grinned as they cast off. "We climbed all three mountains."

As they sailed home Keela closed her eyes to remember the whale they had

seen. As she did, she heard a beautiful sound: a half-whistling, half-singing noise.

"Do you hear the wind in the ropes?" Mali said.

"Mali! That's not the wind!" said Keela. "It's the whale! It's singing to us!"

Mali knew that whales could sing. He also knew what the wind in the ropes sounded like. But he said nothing. He just smiled.

Mali dropped Keela at the castle and sailed back to his island. Wearily he climbed the ladder to his tree-house.

As he dropped into bed he smiled, thinking about the great adventure they'd had that day. And he was asleep before his head even hit the pillow.

DETERMINATION

You focus your energy and efforts on a task and stick with it until it is finished. Determination is using your will power to do something when it isn't easy. You are determined to meet your goals even when it is hard or you are being tested. With determination we make our dreams come true.

Although the climb was difficult and Keela and Mali were tired, they showed great determination to continue up the three mountains. Their determination was rewarded by a feeling of achievement and a wonderous view from the top.

- *Tell me about a time when you have been determined to do something?*
- *What do you think determination would look like if you were learning a new sport or a new musical instrument?*
- *What might happen to your determination if you were to lose your focus? Has this ever happened to you?*
- *Can you think of someone who has shown their determination? What did they do?*
- *What could you do to resist losing your focus when you feel distracted?*

CONSIDERATION

Consideration is being thoughtful of other people and their feelings. You consider how your actions affect them. You pay careful attention to what others like and don't like, and do things that give them happiness.

Even though she was keen to reach the top, Keela told Mali that she wouldn't mind if they needed to go back down instead of carrying on. She was showing consideration for how Mali felt.

- *Can you think of a situation where showing consideration for others would be a good idea?*
- *What are some ways you could show consideration toward a friend or schoolmate?*
- *Do you know someone who might need help or kindness? What could you do for them?*
- *How could you know what the best gift might be for you to give to someone?*
- *Describe yourself doing something considerate for a family member.*

PEACEFULNESS

Peacefulness is being calm inside. Take time for daily reflection and gratitude. Solve conflicts so everyone wins. Be a peacemaker. Peace is giving up the love of power for the power of love. Peace in the world begins with peace in your heart.

———————————— ≈ ————————————

At the top of the third mountain they were "silent in their blue-painted world". They felt at peace as they sat quietly and enjoyed the beauty of the moment.

- *Is there a special place you go to, to enjoy peacefulness?*
- *Do you have a favorite way to practice being peaceful?*
- *How might you achieve a peaceful outcome if you disagreed with your classmate about something and you both thought you were right?*
- *If you saw a fight starting on the playground what could you do to be a peacemaker?*
- *What can you and I do to help create peace in the world?*

TACT

Tact is telling the truth kindly, considerate of how your words affect others' feelings. Think before you speak, knowing what is better left unsaid. When you are tactful, others find it easier to hear what you have to say. Tact builds bridges.

———————————— ≈ ————————————

As they sailed home Mali said, "Do you hear the wind in the ropes?" He knew it was the wind making the whistling sound, but he could see Keela was enjoying the idea that it might be the whale singing to her – he showed tact by choosing to remain quiet.

- *Let's talk about some situations where it would be kind to show tact.*
- *Do you remember a time when you felt embarrassed because someone said something to you without tact? How could they have spoken differently to you?*
- *How would you demonstrate tact if you were standing in line behind someone who looked very different than you?*
- *If your friends were making fun of someone, can you think of a tactful way that you could respond?*

THE STOWAWAY

Caring ⁓ Patience ⁓ Service ⁓ Honesty

*K*eela dangled her feet and watched the little fish below.

A sound made her look up – the flapping of sails as Mali's boat approached the jetty.

Mali threw Keela a rope and then jumped, landing beside her.

"Remember our last visit to Banana Island?" he asked, as he tied up the boat. "We noticed the swing-bridge was broken. Why don't we try to fix it!"

"Great idea!" Keela replied. "I love it there – those monkeys are so funny. And they'll be pleased if we can fix their bridge."

The weather was warm as they sailed to Banana Island. As Mali eased the boat on to the beach they could hear monkeys calling from the trees.

They carried a length of rope to where a swing-bridge drooped over a stream.

"We need to replace that old rope," Mali said as he inspected the bridge.

"And fix those missing planks too," Keela added.

Curious monkeys watched from the trees. Some of them swung down for a closer look. One little fellow crept up and touched Keela's hand. She jumped in surprise.

"Oh, hello," she soothed as the young monkey scuttled away again.

The little monkey watched them work. After securing the new rope, Keela found suitable branches and dragged them into a pile. Mali then cut the branches to size and lashed them to the rope.

"Thank you!" Mali laughed as the little monkey dropped a thin, bent, branch at his feet.

Soon the bridge stood straight and strong again. As they stood back to admire their work the little monkey ran onto the bridge and did a dance in the middle!

"I guess that shows it's strong enough," Keela laughed. "Now, let's explore!"

Over the bridge and up the hill they went.

"Do you hear that?" Mali whispered as they walked. But as soon as they stopped to listen, the sound behind them stopped.

They took two steps.

Rustle rustle.

They stopped.

Silence.

Suddenly a little monkey scampered past and shot up a banana tree.

Plop!

A banana landed at Keela's feet.

Plop! Plop!

Two more bananas rained down.

"Thank you, monkey!" Keela called out as she picked up the bananas.

They ate as they walked. When Keela and Mali stopped, the monkey climbed the nearest tree and waited. When they walked on it swung through the branches. The path took them through the forest, and then back to the swing-bridge.

The monkey stayed with them all the way to the boat, but when they were ready to cast off, he was nowhere to be seen.

"I wonder where our little friend is," Keela said, waving to the monkeys on the beach.

"Off having fun somewhere, I expect," Mali replied, steering his boat back out to the open sea.

They'd sailed nearly all the way home when – *plop!* – a banana landed on the deck at Mali's feet.

Mali looked around. Keela was peering out to sea. Was she playing a trick on him?

Plop!

This time a banana landed on Mali's head! He looked up. A pair of twinkly eyes peeped over the top of the sail.

"Keela!" Mali called. "We've got a stowaway. Look."

"It's the little monkey!" she said. "We'd better take him back – his family will be looking for him."

"Turn around? Oh Keela, we're nearly home!" Mali said.

"I know," Keela answered, "but the other monkeys will be worried. Come on, it won't matter if we have to sail a bit longer."

There was a gathering of monkeys on the beach when they finally arrived back. The little monkey was greeted with noisy excitement.

An adult monkey held out a banana for Mali. He took the banana and nodded his thanks in return.

"We'll see you next time!" Mali called to the young monkey.

But as they turned to leave the little monkey ran and jumped into Mali's arms.

"He doesn't want you to go!" Keela laughed. "You'll have to stay and live with the monkeys!"

"Or he could come and live with me!" Mali replied with a smile.

At that the little monkey leapt up and down with excitement. He jumped down and scampered to where the other monkeys stood. There was much pointing and chatting. An adult monkey checked his head for fleas. Another inspected his teeth and gave him a big, monkey-lipped kiss. The other young monkeys whooped and cheered.

Then, to Mali's surprise, the monkey jumped back on the boat again.

"I think he's taken up the offer to live with you," Keela said.

"Well, a bit of company would be fun," Mali said thoughtfully. "OK – I guess he can always come back if it doesn't work out."

The wind caught the sails as they cast off again. The monkey drummed happily on the side of the boat.

"Keela, he needs a name," Mali said. "Any ideas?"

"Listen – it sounds like he's playing the bongo drums. How about calling him Bongo?"

"Bongo," said Mali, trying out the name. "What do you think, Bongo?"

The little monkey's head bobbed up and down as he drummed even louder.

Bongo explored the boat. He was curious about everything. He pulled on ropes to see what they did. He climbed up the mast and perched at the top.

Suddenly there was a CRASH!

On the deck lay a broken telescope. It was bent and the lens had popped out.

Mali looked up. Bongo was hiding behind the mast.

"Bongo," he said, picking up the pieces. "Did you take my telescope up there?"

Bongo shook his head and then ducked behind the sail.

"This is different from a banana – bananas don't break when you throw them, but things like this do," Mali told him.

He held up the telescope to show Bongo what had happened. "You did throw this, didn't you?"

Bongo climbed down and stood beside Mali. He looked at the broken telescope and then looked up at Mali. He nodded sadly.

"I think I can fix this," Mali said, inspecting the telescope. "It should straighten out, and the lens should fit back in." He rubbed Bongo's head. "I'm glad you're coming to stay with me, but please be careful with my things."

"You need to give him time, Mali," Keela reminded him. "Bongo has a lot to learn."

The sun was setting by the time they dropped Keela at her castle and sailed home.

Mali made up a little monkey-sized bed in the tree-house. As soon as he'd finished Bongo climbed in and fell fast asleep.

"Sweet dreams, little guy," Mali said.

CARING

Caring is giving love and attention to people and things that matter to you. When you care about people, you help them. You do a careful job, giving your very best effort. You treat people and things gently and respectfully. Caring makes the world a safer place.

Mali and Keela care about how the other monkeys might feel when they find Bongo gone, so they take him back to Banana Island. Bongo also learns about needing to take care of Mali's things by treating them gently and respectfully.

- *How do you feel when people show that they care for you?*
- *Can you think of how you might show that you care for others?*
- *What would caring look like when it comes to doing your homework or chores around the house?*
- *How might you show caring to a child on the playground who was running and fell down?*
- *As you are setting the dinner table with your mother's favorite dishes, what would caring look like?*

PATIENCE

Patience is quiet hope and trust that things will turn out right. You wait without complaining. You are tolerant and accepting of difficulties and mistakes. You picture the end in the beginning and persevere to meet your goals. Patience is a commitment to the future.

Mali has to turn the boat around to return Bongo to Banana Island. He is keen to get home and this will take extra time. But Keela reminds him that there is no hurry, and he can be patient about getting home. She reminds him that it's more important to do the right thing than to hurry home.

- *Can you think of a time when you were patient?*
- *When is it most difficult for you to practice patience?*
- *What would patience look like if you were eager to get home and go play with a friend, but you promised to walk your little sister home who walks slower than you?*
- *How could you practice patience if you were trying to build something and it kept collapsing?*
- *Who have you observed practicing patience at home? At school? In your community?*

SERVICE

Service is giving to others, making a difference in their lives. You consider their needs as important as your own; be helpful without waiting to be asked; do every job with excellence. When you act with a spirit of service, you can change the world.

An example of service is when Keela and Mali fix the swing-bridge on Banana Island so that it works better for the monkeys who live there. They were being helpful without being asked.

- *Can you think of examples when you observed someone being of service to another?*
- *What could you do to be helpful without being asked in your community? At school? At home?*
- *What would being of service look like if you were walking down your street and noticed a neighbor's trash can had been knocked over and there was trash spilling out?*
- *Can you share an example of something you could do for someone that could make a difference in their life?*
- *What are examples of times that you were of service to someone? What did that feel like?*

HONESTY

Honesty is being truthful and sincere. It is important because it builds trust. When people are honest, they can be relied on not to lie, cheat, or steal. Being honest means that you accept yourself as you are. When you are open and trustworthy, others can believe in you.

When Bongo broke the telescope, he showed honesty by admitting that he had thrown it.

- *Sometimes it can be uncomfortable admitting that you did something if you think that you might get in trouble. Do you think Bongo did the right thing by being honest? Why?*
- *Do you think it is important to practice honesty? Why or why not?*
- *Has anyone ever been untruthful with you? How did you feel about that person afterwards?*
- *Have you ever been in a situation where it was really hard to be truthful? What made you decide to be truthful or not truthful?*
- *How might honesty help relationships with family and friends to grow strong?*

RESCUE AT DOLPHIN BAY

Kindness ⁓ *Perseverance* ⁓ *Reliability* ⁓ *Detachment*

*T*here was nobody at Dolphin Bay when Keela arrived. She sat on the warm sand and waited.

This is very strange, she thought. *There would be footprints in the sand if Mali had been here.* She looked out to the ocean. *And there's no sign of his boat in the bay.*

"Mali!" she yelled, hoping he might be close enough to hear.

This isn't like him, she thought. *I hope he's all right.*

She looked along the beach again and saw a small brown shape, scampering toward her.

"BONGO? IS THAT YOU?" she yelled, running to the little monkey.

Bongo jumped into her arms.

"What's happened, Bongo? Where's Mali?" she asked.

Bongo jumped down and pointed down the beach toward an outcrop of rocks. He took her hand and tugged.

"OK, I get it... let's go," she told him, running to keep up.

At the end of the beach the rocks towered high above them. Bongo climbed quickly to the top.

"Bongo! Did you find her?" Mali called from the other side.

"Mali!" Keela shouted. "Are you OK?"

"We have a problem," Mali called back. "Can you make it over here?"

She tried to pull herself up the rocks.

Now would be a good time to be a monkey, she thought as her hands slipped and her feet slid. When she finally reached the top she saw what Mali meant.

Mali sat in a rock pool beside a struggling dolphin. Tangled around its tail and body were thick strands of seaweed.

Keela scrambled down to the rock pool.

"Is it hurt?" Keela asked, drawing her hand to her mouth.

"No, I don't think so," Mali replied. "But it is stuck. It must have been feeding on the fish that hide in the kelp." He pointed to the brown leathery seaweed that clung to the rocks beneath the water.

"It was a good thing we spotted him on our way to meet you – much longer without help and he'd have been in real trouble," Mali said.

The dolphin let out a sorrowful sound. Tears filled Keela's eyes as she watched.

"The tide is going out," Mali said as the dolphin struggled in the water beside him. He knew the dolphin would soon overheat if it couldn't get back to the cool deep water.

"What are we going we do?" Keela cried. Her heart pounded in her chest.

"Take a deep breath," Mali said. "To help this little guy we need to keep calm."

Keela tried to control her feelings.

Think, she told herself. *Think, Keela.*

"I've tried freeing him," Mali continued. "But it's no use – he's too tightly tangled. I can't pull the kelp off without hurting him."

Keela took another deep breath. She closed her eyes and thought hard.

"Our first problem is the sun," she said. "We need to keep him cool."

She looked around. There was nothing but rocks. She looked inland and saw a coconut tree growing high above the rocks.

"If Bongo can get one of those palm leaves we can use it to keep the sun off the dolphin," Keela said. "They're big enough to shade him."

While Bongo climbed the rocks to reach the coconut palm, Mali splashed water over the dolphin. He spoke to it soothingly as it floundered in the shallow water.

"See if you can find a coconut," Mali called to Bongo. He turned to Keela. "We could use the shell to scoop water over the dolphin."

At the foot of the tree was a fallen coconut. Bongo picked it up and threw it. It bounced down the rocks and landed near Keela.

"Well done!" Keela shouted.

Bongo quickly climbed the tree. He grabbed hold of a palm leaf and pulled. The leaf stretched and stretched, then it sprung back into place.

"Try another," Keela called. "There might be a loose one."

Bongo tried another and another – each time the same thing happened. The leaves would not come out.

Keela looked down at the rock pool. The dolphin was moving less now, exhausted after struggling in the heat.

"Bongo, you have to keep trying!" she urged. She breathed deeply to calm her feelings.

Bongo tested each leaf again. He tugged and he heaved. He pulled and he twisted. Eventually he found one that was looser than the others. He tugged with all his might and it came free.

Back down again, Bongo presented the coconut leaf proudly to Keela. Together they wedged it between two rocks, casting a cooling shadow over the dolphin.

"Great work," Mali said. "Now we need to make a scoop from that coconut – we can't let the dolphin dry out. Do you think you can split the coconut on that rock, Keela?"

Keela raised the coconut over her head and brought it down with a sharp *crack!* White liquid splashed out as the coconut split in two.

"Coconut milk!" Keela said, licking a drop that landed on her cheek. She picked up a large cup-shaped piece of coconut shell.

"A perfect scoop," she said, dipping it in the rock pool and gently pouring the soothing water over the dolphin.

Mali pointed to a piece of coconut shell that remained on the rock.

"Bongo, pass me that piece there would you?"

Mali tested the edge. It was jagged and sharp. He pushed it against a length of kelp, sawing back and forth. It cut through.

"Keela, look!" Mali said, holding up the kelp.

Mali hacked at the kelp while Keela scooped water over the stricken dolphin. The tide had dropped so much that the rock pool was nearly dry. Finally Mali cut through the last of the binds.

"Careful now," Mali said as they eased the exhausted dolphin out of the rock pool and into water deep enough for it to swim.

The dolphin tested its freedom by turning a few slow circles. He popped his head up and looked back to the friends on the rocks.

"It looks like it's smiling!" Keela said.

The dolphin dived down.

"Where's it gone?" Mali asked, scanning the water.

Suddenly the dolphin leapt out of the water and high into the air. At the top of its jump it did a somersault before diving gracefully down.

"Wow!" laughed Mali and Keela.

The afternoon was spent relaxing at
Dolphin Bay. As Mali and Bongo sailed
home that evening the sun sparkled
on the waves. Beside them a dolphin
swam. Another dolphin, with a smaller
one swimming alongside, joined them. The
dolphins played hide and seek under the boat
and jumped joyfully in the boat's wake.

What a day, Mali thought.

He turned to Bongo.

"I think we'll sleep well tonight, little buddy," he said.

KINDNESS

Kindness is showing you care, doing some good to make life better for others. Be thoughtful about people's needs. Show love and compassion to someone who is sad or needs your help. When you are tempted to be cruel, to criticize or tease, decide to be kind instead.

The friends showed kindness by helping the stranded dolphin. Mali comforted the dolphin with soothing words while they tried to work out how to rescue it.

- *How do you feel when people show kindness to you?*
- *Who do you know who you would say is a kind person? Why?*
- *Can you describe a time when you showed kindness to someone at school? A stranger? A family member? How did you feel afterwards?*
- *What could you do to show kindness to someone who seems sad or lonely?*
- *Name some ways that we can be kind to animals.*

PERSEVERANCE

Perseverance is being steadfast and persistent. You commit to your goals and overcome obstacles, no matter how long it takes. When you persevere, you don't give up...you keep going. Like a strong ship in a storm, you don't become battered or blown off course. You just ride the waves.

It was difficult for Bongo to pick the coconut leaf. He had to keep trying, working hard, until finally he managed to loosen one. He knew it was important, and he didn't give up.

- *Sometimes we have to work really hard to achieve things. Can you think of an example of a time when you showed perseverance to achieve a goal?*
- *Was there ever a time when you wanted to do something or reach a goal but gave up before you did? How did that feel?*
- *If you were doing something you had never done before and were afraid you might fail, how would perseverance help?*
- *Name some people you have seen demonstrate perseverance. What did they do?*

RELIABILITY

Reliability means that others can depend on you. You keep your commitments and give your best to every job. You are responsible. You don't forget, and you don't need to be reminded. Other people can relax knowing things are in your reliable hands.

Mali is always reliable, so it was very strange that he wasn't on the beach where he'd arranged to meet Keela. Keela knew there must have been something wrong – it wasn't like him not to show up.

- *Do you think reliability makes it easier for people to trust you? Why?*
- *Who are the people in your life that you know are reliable? Why?*
- *How do you feel when a person forgets to do what they promised?*
- *What do you think would happen to our pet if we forgot to be reliable?*
- *If you borrowed a friend's toy or bicycle, what could you do to be reliable?*

DETACHMENT

Detachment is experiencing your feelings without allowing your feelings to control you. Instead of just reacting, with detachment you are free to choose how you will act. You use thinking and feeling together, so you can make smart choices.

Keela was getting very upset about the trapped dolphin. She needed to control her feelings so that she could use her head as well as her heart to help.

- *Sometimes we become cross or upset, and it's difficult to feel anything else. Do you think it is possible to have a strong feeling but not be controlled by it?*
- *If you were feeling very angry at a classmate for teasing you, how could you practice detachment before you react?*
- *What are some of the choices you have when someone is teasing or bullying you?*
- *When do you think are the hardest times to practice detachment?*
- *Name a time when you needed a lot of detachment.*

CAMPING WITH THE KING

Humility ⁓ *Assertiveness* ⁓ *Honor* ⁓ *Understanding*

$\mathcal{T}$he royal breakfast table was piled high with exotic fruits and fancy pastries.

"My girl!" said the king, "what *is* the matter?"

Princess Keela looked up. She had been staring at her breakfast, not eating.

"Don't you have everything you need, my blossom?" he continued. "Do you want a new dress? A new tiara perhaps? Would a new pony make you happy?"

"Dad, I don't need more *things* to make me happy," Keela said, looking over at her mother, who encouraged her with a smile. "What I would truly love..."

"Name it, my darling, and it will be yours!" the king interrupted, prodding another pastry into his mouth.

"Well, I would love to go camping. With you. In a tent." Her eyes sparkled as she spoke. She knew that her father had never slept anywhere except in his luxurious castle.

"Camping?" said the king.

"Yes. In a tent," Keela repeated.

"Then we shall go camping!" the king replied. He picked up a bell and rang it loudly. Straightaway there was a servant at the doorway.

"We are going camping," the king announced to the servant. "I need you to find me the biggest tent in the land – a circus big-top would be perfect! We will camp in style!"

"Yes, sir," the servant replied. He clicked the heels of his shoes together and turned to leave.

"Wait!" the king called. "There's more. We'll need the best camper-people in the land. We'll also need map-readers, chefs who are barbeque experts, and people to carry our royal beds so that we can camp in comfort!"

"Yes, sir," the servant repeated. He clicked his heels again and left the room.

"Oh, Daddy," Keela sighed. "I mean *real* camping; just you and me in a little tent that we put up ourselves. We'll hike to our camping spot with everything we need in our backpacks. We'll cook our food over a fire we'll make ourselves..."

"Nonsense!" the king cried. "I wouldn't think of having my little blossom carrying a heavy pack on her pretty royal back. That's what servants are for."

And with that he stood. "Must go... lots to organize with this camping business."

He was off before Keela could say another word.

Keela turned to her mother. The queen could tell that her husband had misunderstood. She had often told Keela about when she was a girl – long before she'd married the king – when she had gone camping with her father. She had told Keela about the smell of smoke in the cold night air. Even the food that she'd burnt had a magical taste because she'd cooked it herself. She'd made the campfire with wood she'd gathered herself. She remembered the safe feeling she had with her father there as she peeked out from the tent to see a night sky glittering with millions of stars. She knew how much Keela loved those stories.

"Keela," she said, "you'll just have to be assertive with him. Tell him exactly what you mean, and keep trying until he finally understands!"

Over the next few days Keela tried to speak with the king. He was so busy ordering his staff around, turning her camping idea into a huge expedition, that she couldn't get him to listen to her.

"Dad!" Keela finally shouted in frustration. The king stopped.

"This is important... I really need you to listen to me."

The king waved away the servant he was instructing. He stood still, ready to listen to Keela for the first time in days.

Although the king couldn't understand why anyone would want to give up their royal comforts, even if it was just for a night or two, he could see how important it was to Keela, so he agreed to her plan.

*

The smoke from the campfire swirled around Keela's head, making her eyes water. The king also had watery eyes even though the smoke was blowing away from him.

"It's beautiful, Keela," he said quietly.

The sun had dipped below the horizon, creating an orange glow beneath the blue-black evening sky. The first stars of the evening were already appearing, glowing like diamonds. The tent made a gentle flapping sound in the evening breeze.

"Do you know, Keela," he continued, "even though my shoulders ache from carrying that pack, it's a good feeling."

Keela nodded in agreement. A cricket chirruped nearby. It seemed to be singing a sunset song.

"Listen to that," the king said. "I'm a king, and he's just an insect, yet it makes no difference to the sunset or the stars or the air that we both breathe... we get to enjoy this beauty as equals."

Keela could tell that this was a special moment for her father. He gazed into the fire with a faraway look in his eyes.

"Thanks, Keela," he said.

"Thank you for listening to me," Keela replied. "It was difficult for you to give up your royal comforts, but you said that you'd come camping with me, and you kept your word."

After watching the sky fill with stars, they put out the fire and crawled into their little tent.

Keela snuggled down into her sleeping bag.

"Dad?" she said.

"Hmmm?"

"It's your birthday soon. You're the king, you can have anything you want. What would make you the happiest?"

The king was quiet for a moment.

"Keela, what would make me happy," he said, "is something more valuable than the biggest diamond in the world. Something way more precious and beautiful..."

Keela looked over to her father.

He continued. "For my birthday I would like... to go camping again."

The king yawned a tired yawn.

"Goodnight, Dad," Keela whispered.

But the king was already asleep.

HUMILITY

Humilty. Being humble is considering others as important as yourself. You are thoughtful of their needs and willing to be of service. You don't expect others or yourself to be perfect. You learn from your mistakes. When you do great things, humility reminds you to be thankful instead of boastful.

The king displays humility when he stops acting like a bossy king and listens to what Keela is saying – recognizing that her view is as important as his. With humility he recognizes that an insect enjoys the same beautiful sunset as he does. In this way he sees the cricket as an equal.

- *Sometimes people can be boastful rather than being thankful. Can you think of a time when it would have been appropriate for you to show humility?*
- *If you had scored the winning goal, how could you demonstrate humility?*
- *What do you think humility would look like if you made a mistake that hurt someone's feelings?*
- *Can you describe a time when you saw someone at school/home demonstrate humility?*
- *What does it feel like to be around someone who always acts like they know more than you?*

ASSERTIVENESS

Being assertive means being positive and confident. You are aware that you are a worthy person with your own special gifts. You think for yourself and express your own ideas. You know what you stand for and what you won't stand for. You expect respect.

The king wasn't listening to Keela. She tried repeatedly to get him to understand her idea of camping, but he was wrapped up in his own ideas. She needed to use assertiveness to ensure he was listening.

- *Have there been times when you have acted with assertiveness?*
- *Saying 'No' to something you don't think is right is being assertive. Can you recall a time when you did this or saw someone else do this?*
- *When you see someone acting like a bully, do you think they are being assertive? Why or why not?*
- *When Keela was assertive with her father, she asserted herself with respect for him. What do you think might have happened if she had acted disrespectfully?*
- *When you are assertive you don't accept unfair or hurtful treatment. Can you describe a time when you saw someone speak up about something that wasn't fair, respectfully?*

HONOR

Honor is living by the virtues, showing great respect for yourself, other people, and the rules you live by. When you are honorable, you keep your word. You do the right thing regardless of what others are doing. Honor is a path of integrity.

———— ≈ ————

The king likes the idea of a huge circus-like tent, and servants to carry his comfortable bed for him. He is reluctant to go camping without these comforts, but displays honor and integrity by keeping his word to his daughter.

- *Can you name some of the honorable people in your life? They could be members of your family, some of your friends, or it could be someone you read about or saw on television. Why do you think they are honorable?*
- *What would honor look like if you told your mom you would do your homework while she ran an errand, but your friend knocks on your door and wants you to go play?*
- *How could you demonstrate honor after you have made a mistake?*
- *How could you respond honorably if a friend dared you to take a candy bar without paying for it?*
- *What kind of behaviors might cause someone to lose their honor?*

UNDERSTANDING

Understanding is using your mind to think clearly, paying careful attention to see the meaning of things. An understanding mind gives you insights and wonderful ideas. An understanding heart gives you empathy and compassion for others. Understanding is the power to think and learn and also to care.

———— ≈ ————

As they talked around the camp fire, the king paid attention to the beauty and simplicity of the experience. Even though his shoulders ached from carrying the pack, he discovered it could be a good feeling. His understanding led to appreciation.

- *How does it feel to you when you recognize that you understand something new? Tell me about a time when you had that feeling.*
- *What do you think the expression "Put yourself in their shoes" means? Have you ever tried to do this?*
- *How easy or difficult is it to understand new information if you are not paying attention?*
- *Describe a time when you used your head to solve a problem. Were you successful? How did that feel?*
- *How might you show empathy for your teacher when she seems irritable?*

GLOW-WORM CAVE

Trust ∽ *Respect* ∽ *Truthfulness* ∽ *Forgiveness*

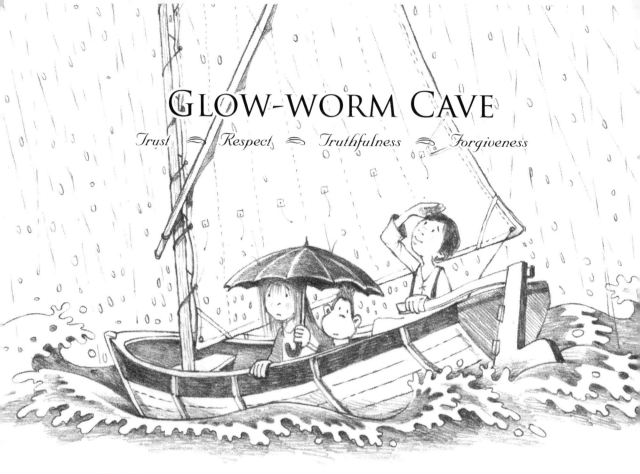

*K*eela and Mali had been planning their adventure to Glow-worm Cave for weeks. Keela pulled back her curtains... and saw fat raindrops splattering against the window. *Oh,* she thought sadly. Wind howled around the tower of the castle.

Her eyes followed a big raindrop as it raced a small drop to the bottom of the windowpane.

"Are you ready?" Mali called from the stairs. As he reached her doorway he added, "It's a great day for an adventure!"

"Mali! Look at the weather!" Keela said. "We'll get drenched if we go out in that!"

"Ah, but look," Mali pointed out the window. "See the clouds making an arch shape on the horizon? That's the wind from the south. This rain won't last long."

Keela knew that Mali spent so much time on his boat he could read the oceans and skies better than anybody.

"Well ... all right, if you *really* think it will clear," she said.

The wind filled the sails of Mali's boat as they cast away from the pier. Keela gripped the side of the boat with one hand and clutched an umbrella with the other. Bongo huddled in beside her. Water was everywhere – splashing up from the sea and beating down from the sky.

Keela's tummy felt jumpy as Mali steered the boat through the lumpy waves.

"You all right?" Mali shouted over the roar of the wind. Keela forced a smile and nodded.

After a while, the ocean started to settle and the rain began to ease. The drumming on Keela's umbrella became quieter. It was soon a gentle tapping, until finally Keela was able to fold her umbrella down altogether.

The arch of blue that Mali had pointed out had grown, until now there was blue sky all around. Keela smiled, marveling at Mali's weather-reading skills.

Bongo climbed the mast and searched out to sea. He pointed excitedly. Keela looked and could just make out the shape of land.

"Mali! An island, straight ahead," she called.

"That'll be Rainbow Atoll," Mali replied.

"Atoll?" Keela asked.

"It's like an island, but it's actually a reef. It's in the shape of a circle and there's a lagoon in the middle." He peered at his map.

"The cave should be on the far side."

Mali found a gap through to the lagoon. The water was crystal-clear and they could see down to the coral at the bottom.

Bongo climbed down the mast and peered over the side.

"What do you see, Bongo?" asked Keela. Her eyes widened as she looked. "Wow!" she said.

Thousands of brightly-colored fish swirled through the water. Bongo poked at them with Keela's folded umbrella. All of a sudden the umbrella sprung open. Bongo let go in surprise, and it dropped to the water.

"Bongo, don't!" Mali shouted as Bongo leapt. It was too late... Bongo landed in the upside-down umbrella, and sailed it as though it was a small boat.

"Use your paws as paddles," Mali shouted. But Bongo paddled with just one paw and the umbrella went round and round in circles. He grinned his monkey smile and waved happily.

Mali shook his head and smiled. "Here, catch this rope Bongo – I'll tow you ashore."

The boat, with umbrella in tow, sailed gently across the lagoon. There were so many colorful fish swirling beneath them it looked like they were floating on a rainbow.

"Ah ha! Here it is," said Mali when they reached the far side. The shadowy shape of a cave appeared.

"I can't wait to see how far it goes!" Mali said, as the boat came to rest on sand at the mouth of the cave.

He reached over and helped Bongo from the umbrella.

Keela leapt to the sand and Mali followed. But rather than jumping down with them, Bongo climbed up the mast.

"What's the matter, Bongo?" Keela asked. "Are you worried about the dark?"

Bongo nodded.

"How about you look after the boat for us, Bongo. We won't be long," Mali assured him. "See you soon."

Keela and Mali scrambled into the cave. They stopped every few minutes to let their eyes adjust to the darkness. As they went deeper, something wondrous appeared.

The rocks above them began to glow with thousands of tiny lights.

"Glow-worms!" Keela exclaimed. "Wow!"

"Whooo hoo!" Mali shouted with joy. "Look at them! They look like stars in the sky... they're amazing! Whooo hooo!!!"

But as Mali shouted, one by one the little lights went out until there were only a few faint dots of light above them.

"Mali," Keela said. "Glow-worms don't like noise."

"But I'm not hurting them, Keela."

"We're in their cave. They might be little, but we still need to respect that this is their home and they like it quiet."

They stood very still. Slowly the little lights began to glow again.

It was cold and damp inside the cave, and soon they were ready to return to the boat.

As they sailed back out of the lagoon again Mali noticed something strange. He had left the umbrella folded up, but now it was open – and full of seawater. Splashing around in the bottom were little rainbow fish.

"Keela, what do you make of this?" he asked.

"It looks like Bongo went fishing while we were away," Keela said, looking up the mast. "Bongo, do you know anything about this?"

Bongo shook his head and tried to hide behind the mast. Mali looked at the little fish struggling in the umbrella.

"Bongo," he said, "these fish live in the lagoon because the water here is warm and they get food and protection from the coral. If these fish are removed they'll probably die."

Bongo climbed down. He stood with Mali and Keela, looking at the fish.

"Did you want to take them back home to live with us at our island?" asked Mali.

Bongo nodded his head.

"I know you didn't want to hurt them, Bongo, but you must return them to the lagoon."

Bongo picked up the umbrella and gently tipped it out over the side of the boat. The fish scurried away in a flash of color.

Mali could see that Bongo felt bad about catching the fish. He held out his hand. "Come on, mate," he said. "Let's set sail for home."

As they sailed home the sun dipped below the horizon. The sky grew dark and stars began to appear in the night sky. Keela felt the warm evening breeze on her skin.

"Mali," she said. "Look up. The stars look just like the glow-worms in the cave."

"We'd better talk quietly then. To make sure they don't go out!"

It had been another magical day for the young adventurers.

TRUST

Trust is having faith in someone or something. It is a positive attitude about life. You are confident that the right thing will happen without trying to control it or make it happen. Even when difficult things happen, trust helps us to find the gift or lesson in it.

Keela decides to trust in Mali's ability to read the weather. Heading off in the rain is unpleasant, but Mali's positive attitude rubs off on Keela. Her trust is rewarded by the most amazing day.

• *Can you think of any examples of trust?*
• *What do you think made Keela find Mali trustworthy?*
• *How do people build trust?*
• *Once you have earned someone's trust how long does it last?*
• *Once you lose trust how easy or difficult is it to regain that trust?*
• *Who are people that you trust and why?*

RESPECT

We show respect by speaking and acting with courtesy. We treat others with dignity and honor the rules of our family, school and nation. Respect yourself, and others will respect you.

Mali and Keela showed respect by keeping quiet in the glow-worm caves – even though they were just worms they were still treated with respect.

• *What are some respectful behaviors you might see at home? At school? For the environment? For yourself? In your community?*
• *What are some good ways to show respect to people you know?*
• *How can you tell if someone respects you?*
• *What are some actions that could lead to loss of respect?*
• *Do you think showing common courtesy relates to respect? How?*

TRUTHFULNESS

Truthfulness is being honest in your words and actions. You don't tell lies even to defend yourself. Don't listen to gossip or prejudice. See the truth for yourself. Don't try to be more than you are to impress others. Be yourself, your true self.

When Mali discovers the fish in the umbrella, Bongo shows truthfulness by admitting that he had collected them to take home.

- *At first Bongo didn't want to admit that he had caught the fish. Do you think he did the right thing by admitting that he did catch the fish? Why?*
- *How do you feel when you know someone has lied to you?*
- *How do you feel about yourself when you have been truthful? When you have told a lie?*
- *Do you think lying could become a habit – something you do without thinking? How would you change that habit?*
- *Describe a time when it was really hard for you to tell the truth.*
- *Why do you think someone might exaggerate the truth about what they did or what they have?*

FORGIVENESS

Being forgiving is giving someone another chance after they have done something wrong. Everyone makes mistakes. Instead of revenge, make amends. Forgive yourself too. Instead of feeling hopeless after a mistake, decide to act differently, and have faith that you can change.

Mali could see that Bongo didn't want to hurt the fish. Once he realized that the fish might die if he took them from the lagoon, Bongo felt bad. He made a mistake, and he learned from it. Mali displayed forgiveness as he held out his hand to Bongo.

- *Can you think of a time when you forgave someone? What did that feel like?*
- *Can you think of a time when someone forgave you? How did that feel?*
- *What might have happened if Mali had blamed or put down Bongo for his mistake?*
- *Can you think of any reason why you would not want to forgive someone? How could you get past that?*
- *Can you recall how you felt in a situation before you forgave someone and how it felt afterwards?*

THE SHOW MUST GO ON!

Commitment ⮌ *Cooperation* ⮌ *Orderliness* ⮌ *Tolerance*

*P*uffing hard, Keela stopped beside her uncle.

"What's the matter, Uncle Philippe?" she asked, kneeling beside him on the grass.

"I twisted my ankle," Philippe said, grimacing with pain.

Keela had been having fun playing chase with her uncle, darting between the large boxes that were arranged in the field behind the castle. Around the boxes teams of workers were unpacking for the circus show that night.

Philippe, as the brother of the king, was once expected to become a royal statesman, running the affairs of the kingdom. But when his royal tutors tried to teach him to count piles of money, he did tricks with the coins. And when the tutors tried to teach him how to write important documents, Philippe drew pictures.

"I'm running away to join the circus!" Philippe had announced one day. Nobody believed him. Until the day a circus passed through. And Philippe joined them.

That was years ago. Philippe visited from time to time, bringing Keela stories of his adventures. He would tell her about exciting foreign lands, and about the long, hard hours of training he had to do to become a brilliant performer.

But right now, seeing Philippe clutching his ankle, Keela was worried.

A pair of dusty boots appeared. Keela looked up to see a small man lift his top hat and mop his sweaty brow.

"Mister Scurvy," Philippe said, trying to stand, "this is my niece, Keela."

The ringmaster grunted as Philippe sat down again, his ankle too sore to stand on.

Scurvy looked at Philippe's ankle then looked at Keela.

"If you," he pointed a chubby finger at Keela, "have caused my star performer to injure himself..."

He glared at her before turning away.

"Kids," he muttered as he stomped off. "Nothing but trouble the lot of 'em – they're all the same."

"Don't worry about Scurvy," Philippe said as Keela helped him back to the castle. "He's not as bad as he likes people to think he is."

In the castle Keela helped to bandage Philippe's ankle.

"Have you been practicing your juggling?" Philippe asked.

"Watch," Keela said. She picked up three bandages and rolled them into balls. Tossing each in the air with one hand, she caught them with the other, before sending them flying again.

"Bravo!" Philippe clapped.

Philippe and Keela were deep in conversation when the king appeared in the doorway. He looked at his brother's bandaged ankle.

"Will we cancel the show then?" the king asked.

"No, no," Philippe said, giving Keela a wink. "The show must go on!"

The afternoon was filled with activity. Performers larked about in the long grass. Musicians practiced, and laughter filled the air. A huge roll of canvas was laid out in position. Pegs and ropes were arranged in rows. Instructions were shouted, and people worked in teams to put up the massive circus tent.

That evening the king and queen walked with great ceremony to the field. Servants and ladies-in-waiting flustered along behind. Following were noble ladies and gentlemen dressed in their finest evening wear. The tent buzzed with excitement.

Backstage, the ringmaster stood with his hands on his hips.

"I don't care if she IS a princess," Scurvy growled. "She's a kid and you know what I think of them."

"You're the boss," Philippe replied. "But I know she can do this..."

Scurvy looked over at Keela, who was juggling balls – unaware she was being watched. He rubbed his chin, thinking hard.

The circus band struck up the first notes of the opening tune.

"Orright," Scurvy grunted. Turning, he pushed aside the curtains and walked to the ring in the middle of the tent.

"LAAADIES AND GENTLEMENNN!" Scurvy boomed. "Your royal highnesses! What a show we have for you tonight!"

The band blasted out a series of notes as a group of tumblers burst into the ring. They tumbled and leapt and balanced on top of each other. In the audience Mali cheered and Bongo clapped.

Then came the trapeze performers, swinging so high that they nearly touched the top of the tent before swooping down and launching themselves through the air. Turning graceful summersaults they flew across the tent to be caught on the other side by strong swinging arms.

The show continued with one skillful act after another until finally the ringmaster took center ring again.

"For our final act we have the Amaaaazing PHILIPPE!" Scurvy announced and the crowd cheered wildly.

"But," Scurvy held up a hand to quieten the crowd, "this afternoon Philippe had an accident and can't do his usual performance."

The crowd shifted awkwardly.

"So also tonight," the ringmaster continued, "for the first time ever, we bring you... THE INCREDIBLE PHILIPPE *AND* KEEELAAA!"

Trumpets blared and the spotlight swung around. Beside Philippe a small figure stood blinking in the bright light.

Keela put her hand above her eyes to shield them from the glare and saw in the crowd the king and queen smiling back at her. Mali was there too, clapping loudly. Beside him Bongo jumped up and down on his seat.

"Are you ready?" Philippe asked, placing a hand on her shoulder for support.

Keela nodded. She walked slowly as Philippe hopped painfully beside her to the center of the tent. The crowd hushed.

A drum roll shattered the silence.

Philippe balanced on his one good leg, and Keela took three steps back. She threw a ball across the gap to Philippe, then another, and another. Catching each, Philippe tossed them high in the air, juggling while hopping on one foot. Keela threw more balls until Philippe had six balls whirling above him. The crowd cheered.

Philippe tossed one, two, then three balls back to Keela. She caught every one and then sent them flying into the air above her. They were juggling three balls each, and Philippe was now hopping around the ring as he juggled! The crowd burst into rapturous applause again.

And then, Keela dropped a ball.

She carried on juggling with two balls.

She heard Mali call out, "Bongo! No!"

From the corner of her eye she saw Bongo, scampering toward her.

The little monkey snatched up the ball from the ground. He then climbed up her legs and over her back until he was standing on her shoulders. From there he dropped the ball back down into her hands. Keela didn't skip a beat and continued juggling with all three balls.

The crowd cheered, and Bongo grinned widely. The sight of a girl juggling with a monkey on her shoulders drew thunderous applause from the crowd.

Holding hands with Philippe and Bongo, Keela gave a low bow.

After the show Mali went to find Keela backstage. He poked his head between the curtains.

"Hi!" Keela called, seeing Mali's head appear. She waved him over.

As Mali pushed the curtains aside his hand knocked a box of juggling balls. They rolled all over the floor.

Scurvy filled his lungs, ready to yell at Mali.

Kids! He thought. *Nothin' but trouble...* But then he checked himself. *Hang on, I guess the final act was saved by a kid.*

Scurvy paused. He watched Mali pick up the balls.

As Mali dropped the last ball back in the box, Scurvy sighed and nodded towards Keela.

"She was pretty good tonight wasn't she?" he said.

"Pretty good?" Mali replied. He smiled at Keela. "She was BRILLIANT!"

COMMITMENT

Commitment is caring deeply about something or someone. It is deciding carefully what you want to do, then giving it 100%, holding nothing back. You give your all to a friendship, a task, or something you believe in. You finish what you start. You keep your promises.

Uncle Philippe had to train for a long time, practicing hard and giving his full commitment to become good enough to perform with the circus.

- *Why do you think Philippe committed his time and energy to his practice?*
- *Do you think you can become excellent at something without committing yourself to it? Why or why not?*
- *How do you choose what promises you make?*
- *Is there something or someone you feel committed toward? How do you show your commitment?*
- *What would commitment look like when you are doing your homework or a house chore?*

COOPERATION

Cooperation is working together and sharing the load. When we cooperate, we join with others to do things that cannot be done alone. We are willing to follow the rules which keep everyone safe and happy. Together we can accomplish great things.

Teams of people worked together to set up the circus for the performance. It was with cooperation that the tumblers and the acrobats could complete their performances, working with others to accomplish great things.

- *Tell me about the times when you've cooperated with others.*
- *Cooperation means agreeing to follow common rules. What might happen if we didn't cooperate with each other in the classroom? Or on the roads?*
- *Can you think of any famous people who have achieved greatness through cooperation?*
- *What are some things that you can do with others that you could not do by yourself?*
- *How could you be cooperative with someone you were in disagreement with?*

ORDERLINESS

Orderliness is being neat and living with a sense of harmony. You are organized, and you know where things are when you need them. Solve problems step by step instead of going in circles. Order around you creates order inside you. It gives you peace of mind.

To set up for the show, the circus troop needed to be very organized and orderly. They lay the equipment out in an orderly way, setting up step by step.

- Do you think the process of setting up would run smoothly if the troop were disorderly? Why or why not?
- How does it feel when you put your room in order after it's been messy and disorderly?
- How do you think orderliness might apply to your schoolwork?
- Describe a project or activity you did where you demonstrated orderliness?
- Can you give an example of how orderliness can help solve a problem?

TOLERANCE

Being tolerant is accepting differences. You don't expect others to think, look, speak, or act just like you. You are free of prejudice, knowing that all people have feelings, needs, hopes, and dreams. Tolerance is also accepting things you wish were different with patience and flexibility.

At the beginning Mr. Scurvy was unfriendly to Keela just because she is a child. By saying "nothing but trouble the lot of 'em – they're all the same" he showed his prejudice and intolerance. But in the end he exhibited tolerance.

- Was the ringmaster being fair when he said that all kids are nothing but trouble? Why or why not?
- At the end the ringmaster chose not to shout at Mali. What do you think made him act with tolerance?
- You are on a school field trip and the bus you are riding on is very hot and crowded. How do you practice tolerance in this situation?
- Describe a time when you could have practiced more tolerance than you did. How did you feel?
- Have you ever wished that a person would be or act different than they do? How do you practice tolerance in this situation?

MEETING LAO

Integrity ～ *Idealism* ～ *Friendliness* ～ *Self-discipline*

"I'm sure I saw smoke," Keela said as she ran with Mali and Bongo up the soft sand.

Mali and Keela had talked about exploring the little island for a long time. So when Keela spotted a wisp of smoke as they sailed past, they decided to investigate.

From the edge of the beach they found a rough path leading through the trees. Following it, they eventually came to a bamboo hut.

"Someone lives here!" Mali said, noticing the colorful flowers planted on either side of the open front door.

"Anybody home?" Keela called.

At that moment there was a loud *BOOM!* from behind the hut.

"Oh *NO!*" a voice cried out. "Not again."

Behind the hut clouds of dust floated. Boxes, buckets, pots, pipes, and all sorts of equipment were scattered around.

"HELLOOO," yelled Mali.

"Over here," came a shaky voice.

They ran over to a large overturned wooden crate. Peering through the gaps, Mali found that he was staring at the wrinkled face of an old man.

"Are you OK?" Mali asked.

"Not hurt," the old man said. "Just trapped."

Together Mali and Keela tried to lift the crate. They heaved – but it wouldn't budge.

"What happened?" Keela asked, looking around at the mess.

"This thing tipped right over me," the old man answered, "when my experiment went wrong."

"Experiment? You're a scientist?" Mali asked with wonder.

"An inventor," the man replied. "My name is Lao."

Mali and Keela introduced themselves.

"And this is Bongo," Keela added as Bongo reached in to feel Lao's long grey beard.

"Nice to meet you," Lao chuckled as he gave Bongo's paw a friendly shake.

They tried again to lift the crate.

"This is too heavy," Mali said.

"Maybe we can lever it up," Keela suggested.

Searching among the mess they found a plank of wood. Keela shoved one end into the side of the crate and put an upturned bucket under the middle of the plank.

They pushed with all their might on the end. The plank groaned. The crate lifted a tiny bit... then the plank broke with a loud *SNAP!* sending them tumbling to the ground.

"Don't worry," Mali panted. "We'll free you somehow."

Mali looked around. A huge tree grew nearby. He looked up at the branches that reached out overhead.

"Hmmm," Mali pondered. "Bongo, there's a rope on the boat... do you think you can get it?"

Bongo pounded his chest and scuttled off down the path.

While they waited for Bongo to return, Mali and Keela bombarded Lao with questions. What an interesting find he was!

"This island is my home now," Lao told them. "But I used to live on the mainland."

Lao told them how he once owned a big factory. He worked long and hard, but pollution from the factory was making people ill.

"I realized I had to close down the factory before anyone got seriously sick," Lao said. "But the factory was making a lot of money – people said I was crazy to shut it down."

Mali and Keela sat spellbound by the old man's story.

"But I closed it down and moved to this island. From then on I promised to only invent things that would help people. I was working on a water purifier," Lao said, "when I had this wee mishap."

Just then Bongo came scuttling along the path, dragging a long rope behind him.

"Well done, Bongo!" Mali said. "If we can throw the rope over that branch up there," he pointed, "we'll be able to make a pulley to lift the crate."

Mali held one end of the rope. He coiled the rest of it and threw it as hard as he could. It sailed up towards the branch, but instead of dropping down the other side, it stayed up.

Mali tugged. The rope became even more entangled.

Bongo pulled on the rope too. Instead of the rope coming down, Bongo's feet left the ground.

"Hey, yes, that's it! Keep going, Bongo," Mali urged.

Bongo kept pulling; hand over hand, rising all the way up, until he stood on the branch high above them.

"Great! Now see if you can untangle it," Mali called.

There was much shaking and bouncing until finally Bongo proudly held up the freed rope.

"Now hold on to the rope and jump down the other side," Mali called to him. "I'll keep the rope tight and lower you down."

Mali let the rope out slowly, and Bongo floated gently down.

"What a team!" Lao chuckled. "Entertainers as well as rescuers!"

With the rope now slung over the branch, Mali secured it to the crate.

Together they pulled – Keela at the front, Bongo in the middle, and Mali at the back. Slowly the crate began to rise.

"That's it," Lao urged. "Just a bit more."

They heaved with all their might, and the crate lifted slowly. Lao was just about to squeeze out from under it when the branch let out a loud *CREAK!* The weight of the crate was making the branch bend. Suddenly the gap became smaller.

"Just a bit more and I'll be able to squeeze through," Lao said.

Keela's arms ached with the strain. Sweat formed on Mali's brow. The branch creaked again.

Once more they pulled hard, and the crate rose.

As quickly as his old body would allow, Lao wriggled through the gap. Just as he rolled free, the branch broke, sending the crate crashing to the ground.

"Phew!" Lao said, getting to his feet. "That was close!"

"Any damage?" Mali asked.

Lao took a few tentative steps.

"Everything seems to be working," he said.

Back at the hut Lao offered drinks and coconut cookies to all. He told them more about his life. Afterwards, Mali and Keela helped Lao pick up the equipment outside. While they gathered up the pieces Lao explained about his experiment.

"Imagine – clean drinking water for everyone," Lao said.

He looked around at the mess. "It might take me a while, but I'll get this to work."

Mali and Keela found that the afternoon went quickly in the company of their new friend. As the sun began to drop in the sky Lao walked them back to their boat.

"Come and visit any time," Lao called as they cast off.

Wind filled the sails as they waved goodbye.

"Keela," Mali said, staring out to sea. "I wonder what we could invent!"

The sail home was unusually quiet, as Mali and Keela were deep in thought – their minds full of new and exciting ideas.

INTEGRITY

Integrity is living by your highest values. It is being honest and sincere. Integrity helps you to listen to your conscience, to do the right thing, and to tell the truth. You act with integrity when your words and actions match. Integrity gives you self-respect and a peaceful heart.

Lao listened to his conscience and closed down his factory even though it was making a lot of money. He had the integrity to see that the health of other people was more important than making money. He chose to live by his highest values.

- *Acting with integrity is when we listen closely to our conscience and do the right thing. Can you name anyone, either in our society or from the past, who is well known for their integrity?*
- *Integrity means standing up for what you believe in. Describe a time when you stood up for something you believed in.*
- *What would integrity look like if you were taking a difficult test and the teacher leaves the room?*
- *You are walking down the street and you see a person unknowingly drop some money. How would you act with integrity in that situation?*

IDEALISM

When you have ideals, you really care about what is right and meaningful in life. You follow your beliefs. You don't just accept things the way they are. You make a difference. Idealists dare to have big dreams and then act as if they are possible.

Lao chose to spend his time dedicated to making the world a better place. He promised to "only invent things that helped people". He wanted to invent a water purifier so that people could have clean water to drink – then he took action to turn that dream into a reality.

- *What things do you care about that make you want to act to make a difference?*
- *What people do you know of who practice idealism by making a difference? How?*
- *What kinds of things would you need to do to make a "dream" (something important to you) come true?*
- *What are three things people could do to make a difference in our community?*
- *What would an ideal world look like to you? What kinds of actions could help create this world?*

FRIENDLINESS

Friendliness is being a friend, through good times and bad. You take an interest in other people and make them feel welcome. You share your belongings, your time and yourself. Friendliness is the best cure for loneliness.

Lao showed friendliness towards Mali, Keela and Bongo. He made them feel welcome, offering drinks and snacks, and invited them to visit often.

• *How does it feel when people show friendliness towards you?*
• *If you were in a place where you didn't know anyone, what could you do to demonstrate friendliness?*
• *What would a friend do if they saw someone who seemed sad or upset?*
• *What do you find easy about being friendly? What seems difficult for you?*
• *If you wanted to have more friends, what are some things you could do?*
• *If someone new joined your class, how would it make them feel if you showed friendliness toward them? How would they feel if people weren't friendly?*

SELF-DISCIPLINE

Self-discipline means self-control. It is doing what you really want to do, rather than being tossed around by your feelings like a leaf in the wind. You act instead of react. You get things done in an orderly and efficient way. With self-discipline, you take charge of yourself.

When Lao was younger he displayed self-discipline by working hard, building up a successful business. Then he showed self-discipline by deciding to leave the comfort of a rich man's life, to live in a bamboo hut on an island.

• *Self-discipline requires effort. Have there been times when you've had to be self-disciplined to complete something, even though you wanted to go and do something else?*
• *What would self-discipline look like if your brother or sister did something that made you feel very angry?*
• *What are some ways you might use self-discipline when doing your schoolwork?*
• *What would self-discipline look like if you wanted to change a behavior, for example, watching too much TV or spending too much time playing computer games.*
• *Name a few jobs or tasks that require self-discipline for you to do.*

THE HORSE RACE

Enthusiasm   ∾   *Cleanliness*   ∾   *Gentleness*   ∾   *Trustworthiness*

*I*n the royal stables everything was clean and tidy. Saddles and bridles hung in rows. There were neat piles of hay, as well as bins of oats, chaff, and apples. The floor was swept, and everything was in its place.

"Where we're going today is one of my favorite places," Keela told Mali as they prepared. "I'll show you where we can find the juiciest berries you'll ever taste!"

"Here," she continued, handing Mali an apple. "Hold this on the palm of your hand, and let Sandy eat it." She rubbed the neck of a beautiful light-brown horse.

The horse's lips felt soft on Mali's palm. As the horse chomped happily, Mali looked around and thought how tidy the stables seemed compared to his messy tree-house.

"Sandy's really nice to ride," Keela told Mali. "How about you ride him, and I'll take Nutmeg."

She showed Mali how to secure the saddles and adjust the stirrups.

"It's a long way up!" Mali said as he struggled to hoist himself into the saddle.

Keela smiled. She took one step and was up in an instant.

"...And it's a long way down!" he said nervously from the saddle.

They rode the horses slowly to the edge of the woods.

"You're doing really well, Mali," said Keela. "Let's try trotting now. Hold on to the front of your saddle like this." She urged Nutmeg faster by squeezing her legs.

"Whoa, this is bumpy," Mali laughed.

"Great, isn't it?" Keela called, easing Nutmeg along the path that now led into the forest.

Soon they came to a stream where the horses paused to drink from the cool clear water. Mali held on tight as his horse scrambled up the bank on the far side. He grinned. Keela was right, Sandy was fantastic to ride.

Mali's confidence grew as they rode.

"This is it!" Keela announced as they came to a clearing. The sun was bright as they emerged from the trees. Long grass waved in the breeze, and around the edges of the clearing were bushes covered in juicy berries.

The horses grazed on the sweet grass while Mali and Keela collected berries.

"Mmmm," Mali said as juice dripped down his chin. "These are delicious!"

Just then a noise came from the far side of the clearing. Mali's horse threw its head high and rolled its eyes.

"Steady, Sandy... easy now," said Mali as he moved slowly

toward the frightened horse. He could see a thorny branch from a berry bush tangled around its legs.

"That's a good boy," he soothed. "You stand still now."

He held the bridle firmly. He rubbed the horse's nose, and whispered in its ear. Then he bent down and gently removed the thorny branch.

"He got a fright," Keela said to Mali as she came to join him. "But it doesn't look like he's hurt. Mali you were fantastic with him. Well done."

They collected berries a while longer then lazed about in the long grass. They watched clouds change shape as they slid across the sky.

"Hey! There's one that looks like a rabbit," Mali said, pointing.

"Now it looks like it's a whale," Keela added, as the cloud moved above them.

They watched the clouds as the horses grazed happily. After a while they agreed it was time to go.

Mounting up was a lot easier this time around.

"Do you think we can beat them home?" Mali whispered to his horse, giving its neck a rub.

He urged Sandy forward.

"Hey!" Keela said in surprise, as Mali took off.

"Come on," she said to Nutmeg. "Let's catch them."

Nutmeg pricked her ears and stretched out her neck. Her strides grew longer, and her hooves pounded the ground. Keela drew up beside Mali. She smiled, then passed right by – laughing with delight as she took the lead.

"Come on! Faster boy!" Mali urged as his arms flapped at the reins. "Go, Sandy, go!"

Sandy caught up to Nutmeg as they pounded along the forest track side by side. Keela and Mali whooped with joy.

Keela shouted above the noise of the wind and the hooves, "Remember the stream, Mali!"

Keela slowed Nutmeg down by pulling on the reins, and Mali shot ahead, galloping straight towards the stream.

Mali considered pulling the reins to get Sandy to stop too, but

instead, he held on tight. He could feel the horse's powerful body beneath him as he leapt. It felt like they were flying through the air for a very long time. Then they landed – *ker–lop!* – on the far side of the stream.

"We jumped right over it! Did you see that?" Mali called back to Keela.

He turned in time to see Nutmeg and Keela leap the stream too.

Keela beemed with happiness as Nutmeg came to a stop beside Sandy.

"That was fantastic!" Mali said. He patted his hot, sweaty horse.

Keela's heart pounded in her chest.

"We'd better walk the rest of the way to let the horses cool off," she said.

Back at the stables they took off the saddles and bridles. The horses had a lovely roll on the ground.

"They sure look funny waving their feet in the air like that," Mali laughed.

"We need to wash the mud off them and rub them down now," Keela said.

Mali and Keela gave the horses a good clean-down. Then Keela fed them, while Mali hung up the saddles and bridles. Mali liked the smell of horse and hay and leather in the stables. He also liked the way everything was in its proper place.

It's time for a tidy-up here, Mali thought when he arrived back at his tree-house. He whistled as he washed. He sang as he swept. He scrubbed and he tidied.

Afterwards he bathed, washed his hair, and put on clean clothes. He then looked proudly around his clean tree-house.

Through the window he could see clouds scuttling past. One cloud looked just like a horse jumping over a stream.

What a great day, he thought to himself.

ENTHUSIASM

Enthusiasm is being cheerful, happy, and full of spirit. It is doing something wholeheartedly and eagerly. When you are enthusiastic, you have a positive attitude. Enthusiasm is being inspired.

Keela loves her horses. She is enthusiastic about looking after them and takes pride in ensuring they're well cared for. She is also an enthusiastic rider, and when Mali challenges her to a race she rides with great joy and spirit. At the end of the day Mali cleans his house with enthusiasm.

- *What are you enthusiastic about? How do you feel when you approach things with enthusiasm?*
- *Who chooses whether you are enthusiastic or not?*
- *Is there an activity or chore you don't feel enthusiastic about? Can you think of an imaginative way to approach it to create enthusiasm?*
- *How can you tell if a person is enthusiastic? Describe what an enthusiastic person might act like?*
- *When you feel bored, what helps you get your enthusiasm back?*

CLEANLINESS

Cleanliness means washing often, keeping your body clean, and wearing clean clothes. It is putting into your body and your mind only the things that keep you healthy. It is staying free from harmful drugs. It is cleaning up mistakes and making a fresh start.

Keela is careful to ensure the horses are cleaned and looked after. She also makes sure the stables are clean and tidy. Mali realizes that he needs to take more care with cleanliness, and when he does have a good clean-up he feels great.

- *Can you explain the feeling you have when you've just had a bath?*
- *Do you think your surroundings also make a difference to how you feel?*
- *What kinds of things can you put in your body to make sure your body stays healthy and clean?*
- *Can you give an example of a mistake you made that you cleaned up?*
- *What kinds of things can you do to help keep your space at home clean? At school? In your community?*

GENTLENESS

Gentleness is moving wisely, touching softly, holding carefully, speaking quietly and thinking kindly. When you feel mad or hurt, use your self-control. Instead of harming someone, talk things out peacefully. You are making the world a safer, gentler place.

Mali is very gentle with his horse as he untangles its leg from the thorns. By acting with gentleness he makes the horse feel safe and calm.

- *Can you think of a time when someone has acted with gentleness toward you? How did it make you feel?*
- *Can you think of an example where it would be helpful to act with gentleness?*
- *If your friend is wrestling or playing roughly with you, what could you do to play more gently?*
- *What are some things you need to remember if you want to handle something gently?*
- *What would your voice sound like if you wanted to speak gently to someone? What words might you use?*

TRUSTWORTHINESS

Trustworthiness is being worthy of trust. People can count on you to do your best, to keep your word and to follow through on your commitments. You do what you say you will do. Trustworthiness is a key to success in anything you do.

Keela's parents are able to trust Keela with the responsibility of looking after the horses. Keela demonstrated trustworthiness by working hard in the stables and taking good care of the wellbeing of the horses.

- *Who is trustworthy that you know? Why is this person trustworthy?*
- *Can you think of an example of being a trustworthy friend?*
- *In what ways have you practiced trustworthiness?*
- *Do you think it is important that people are trustworthy? Why?*
- *In order to be trustworthy, what would you need to consider before you make a promise?*

KEELA'S SURPRISE

Creativity ⁓ *Generosity* ⁓ *Love* ⁓ *Unity*

"*O*ne week till Keela's birthday!" Mali announced as he jumped out of bed. Bongo scratched his belly and rolled over in his little bed.

"Come on, Bongo," Mali urged. "Let's check the sunflowers in the garden."

Bongo rolled once more, and *THUMP!* he landed, a furry bundle, on the floor.

The seeds Mali had planted months ago had grown beautifully. He'd worked out the best time to plant them so that they would flower in time for Keela's birthday. He had watered them and cared for them, and they had grown into the biggest, sunniest flowers he had ever seen. Mali was feeling very pleased with himself.

But then Mali looked out his window.

"Oh nooooo!" he shouted. Where yesterday a neat row of sunflowers stood proudly, a jumble of leaves and broken stems now lay.

Mali ran down to the garden.

"Oh, Bongo – look," Mali said, shaking his head in disbelief. Parrots squawked loudly in the trees.

"Those parrots have destroyed the sunflowers," said Mali, pointing. "They were after the seeds from the flower heads and they've broken the stems right off." He scooped up a few seeds that were lying in the dust.

"What do I have to give Keela for her birthday now?" Mali said sadly. "She's a Princess. She has nearly everything."

Bongo didn't like seeing Mali sad. He pulled the corners of his mouth out wide and did a funny dance. That usually made Mali smile, but not today.

Later Mali went to talk to his old friend Lao about the parrots and the sunflowers.

"Those parrots were just doing what parrots do best – finding food," old Lao told him.

Lao smiled at Mali. "Now, what are you good at? Everybody has talents – use your talents to create something else for Keela."

"Hmm," said Mali, thinking hard. "I can sail my boat, but Keela and I have already had plenty of sailing adventures. I'm good at gardening, but the sunflowers are no good now."

As he pondered, Mali hummed a little tune.

"What's that tune?" Lao asked.

"It's just a tune that popped into my head," Mali said. "Hey, that's something else I'm good at – I always seem to have a tune in my head."

"Well there you are then," Lao exclaimed. "The perfect birthday gift!"

"But how can I give her a song?" Mali asked.

Suddenly his eyes widened as a brilliant idea came to him. "We could make a band! We could give her a birthday song!"

Lao smiled as he waved goodbye. Mali was so pleased he'd come to visit Lao. He now had a great new plan.

"Thanks, Lao," he yelled.

*

"We've done well, Bongo," said Mali as he placed the last home-made instrument on the bed. There were coconuts filled with crushed shells that made a swishing sound like waves on the shore. There were drums made from hollowed-out logs and a flute made from bamboo. Leaning up against the bed was a guitar-like instrument, with stretched vines for strings.

Mali shook a large seed pod.

"It sounds like rain on banana leaves!" he said.

Bongo beat his chest happily.

"And of course we have your body-drum too," Mali laughed.

*

A few days later it was Keela's birthday. Mali, Bongo and Lao sailed to Keela's castle. But instead of mooring at the jetty as usual, Mali navigated to a small rocky inlet that couldn't be seen from the castle.

When the boat was tied up, the strange band of musicians scurried along the path to the back of the castle, where they were met by the king.

Up in the top tower, Keela sat on her bed and sighed.

Even Mali has forgotten my birthday, she thought sadly. *Even my father.*

"Even my mother!" she said out loud.

"Yes, dear?" said the queen as she entered, hiding a smile behind her hand. "Lovely day isn't it?"

Keela looked at her. *Surely* she had remembered what day it was. Her own mother wouldn't have forgotten her birthday, would she?

The queen walked over to the window. "Why don't we let in some fresh air."

"Mother!" said Keela in frustration. "Have you forgotten something?"

"I don't think so, dear," the queen answered casually. She pushed the window wide open.

As the morning air wafted into the room, strange sounds were carried in with it.

Shhh... crash!... quiet!... over here... not there Bongo!... shhh!!... look, the window's opening!... shhhhh!

Keela glanced at her mother.

"Must be off," the queen said quickly. She dashed from the room faster than Keela had ever seen her move before. Keela heard her skip down the stairs and fly out the back door.

Keela ran to the window. She looked out to the pier, expecting to see Mali's boat tied up, but it wasn't there. Mali HAD forgotten!

From below the window came, *"One, two, three, four..."*

Keela glanced down.

"Happy Birthday, Keeee laaaa!" floated up.

Mali was strumming a weird-looking guitar, while Bongo shook a coconut with so much enthusiasm his whole body bounced up and down with it. There was wise old Lao with a bamboo flute, and even the king and queen were there – waving shakers up and down!

And spread out in front of them was the strangest sight Keela had ever seen – a line of colorful parrots using their beaks to strike a row of drums made from logs. As the parrots dipped their heads to play the drums, the feathers on their heads waved in time, flickering from yellow to orange to red. They looked as beautiful as they sounded!

Keela gasped. "You did remember!"

When the first song finished Keela clapped and clapped.

"Happy birthday, Keela!" Mali called up to her. "Here's our birthday gift to you."

Lao readied the band for the next song. A single note on the flute was joined by a strum from Mali's guitar. More flute notes followed as the drums and shakers joined in. The music built and soared and then – oh how Keela's heart filled with joy at this – they all started singing.

The king's rich bass tones were joined by Lao's harmony, and the queen's sweet voice spread like honey over the top. Mali sang the melody and Bongo added funny ooo-oooh's as he beat his chest in time.

The song finished. Keela beamed. She ran down the stairs two at a time and out the back door to the lawn. She gave them each a big hug.

"Thank you so much," Keela said. "I thought you'd all forgotten my birthday. The surprise was BRILLIANT."

"Actually, I do have something else as well," Mali said, passing her a small package.

Keela opened the bundle. "Seeds?" she asked.

"Inside each seed is a sunflower waiting to come out," Mali laughed.

"And when the sunflowers do come out," Keela said, "I'll remember today... and the best birthday present ever – your song!"

CREATIVITY

Creativity is the power of imagination. It is discovering your own special talents. Dare to see things in new ways and find different ways to solve problems. With your creativity, you can bring something new into the world.

~

Mali wanted to give Keela the perfect birthday present. He knew her parents were able to buy her anything, but he also knew that Keela values thoughtfulness more than anything that can be bought. He displays creativity by coming up with the perfect gift for her.

- *In what other ways did you see creativity displayed in this story?*
- *Can you think of a person who did something creative that made a big difference in your life?*
- *What kinds of creative things do you see your mother do? Your father? Your teacher? Your friend?*
- *Is there a talent that you would like to have? How could you develop that talent?*
- *Have you ever invented anything? Do you know someone who has invented something? What was it?*

GENEROSITY

Generosity is giving and sharing. You share freely, not with the idea of receiving something in return. You find ways to give others happiness, and give just for the joy of giving. Generosity is one of the best ways to show love and friendship.

~

Mali had been planning the perfect gift for a long time. He had watered and tended to the sunflowers. He spent a long time making instruments. Mali, and all of Keela's friends, showed generosity by giving their time and talents to ensure Keela had a wonderful birthday.

- *Can you think of ways to show generosity to people around you?*
- *Describe a situation when you gave your time to help someone who needed it.*
- *If someone in your class forgot their lunch and had no money, how could you show generosity?*
- *How does it feel when someone shares with you? When someone doesn't share with you?*
- *What might you give your best friend if it was their birthday and you had no money? Your mother? Your father?*

LOVE

Love is a special feeling that fills your heart. You show love in a smile, a kind word, a thoughtful act or a hug. Love is treating people and things with care and kindness because they mean so much to you. Love is contagious. It keeps spreading.

Putting on a concert was how the friends showed to Keela their love for her. It was a lovely thing to do and made her feel special and cared for.

- *Tell me about when someone has shown you that they love you. How did you feel?*
- *What are some ways you treat animals lovingly?*
- *How do you show your love to family members?*
- *When you share your love, what do you find usually happens?*
- *Are there other things that you love besides people and animals? What are they?*

UNITY

Unity helps us work and live together peacefully. We feel connected with each other and all living things. We value the specialness of each person as a gift, not as a reason to fight or be scared. With unity we accomplish more together than any one of us could alone.

The friends made beautiful music together. Each person brought their own special talent; there were high voices, low voices and instruments with different sounds, but when they all joined in unity they sounded wonderful together.

- *Can you think of a time when you've worked with others to achieve something?*
- *How are you and your best friend different? The same?*
- *Have you ever been left out of a group or activity you really wanted to be in? How did that feel?*
- *Is there someone you know who looks or acts different than you? Think of that person and name some things that are similar between the two of you.*
- *What would the world be like if everyone looked the same and if everyone thought the same way?*

THE MISSING NECKLACE

Justice ∽ *Loyalty* ∽ *Confidence* ∽ *Compassion*

$\mathcal{K}$eela ran along the jetty to meet Mali.

"Oh Mali," she cried. "Ruby's in trouble."

"Ruby? The maid?" Mali asked. "What's happened?"

"She was cleaning my parents' room," Keela explained. "She held my mother's necklace – just to admire it. Then afterwards, the necklace was gone."

"They think she stole it?" Mali asked.

Keela nodded, then added crossly, "But I don't – she wouldn't do such a thing."

"But if she didn't," Mali asked, "then who did?"

In the kitchen, over a cup of hot cocoa, Keela told Mali how Ruby had opened the window to let in fresh air. After admiring the necklace she had put it back on the dresser, and then finished cleaning the room.

"Only moments later my mother went to put it on – and it was gone!" Keela added. "There was no time for anyone else to have gone in there."

"Maybe it dropped on the floor – under the dresser, or under the bed?" Mali suggested.

"The whole room was searched," Keela replied, shaking her head sadly.

"What about outside the window?" Mali asked. "Perhaps a thief reached through the open window."

"Mali, the window is on the second floor! Nobody would be tall enough."

Keela led Mali outside. Standing under the window Mali could see that Keela was right.

"Maybe they had a ladder," Mali suggested. "But if they did,

they would have left marks," he added, inspecting the grass at their feet.

"There's nothing here but this," Keela said, picking up a black feather.

Suddenly a thought struck her.

"A bird!" she said.

Mali inspected the feather.

"I've heard that crows like shiny things," he said.

In the living room the queen shook her head.

"I know you love Ruby, dear, but… " she looked at the king.

"Crows don't really steal shiny things, Keela," the king said. "That only happens in stories."

Keela walked through the gardens with Mali. At the pond where Ruby was fond of throwing crusts to the ducklings, Keela sighed heavily.

"There's got to be a way to prove she's innocent," Keela said sadly.

Mali scratched his head. He rubbed his chin. There had to be a way.

"To prove Ruby's innocent," Mali began, "we need to prove that a crow could've stolen the necklace."

His eyes widened as he spoke. "So let's leave something shiny out and see if a crow takes it!"

"And if it does, then we can follow it back to its nest," Keela said, "where we'll find the necklace!"

The pair excitedly placed a shiny coin on the lawn and hid behind a bush.

They waited. And waited. It had seemed a good idea, but, crouching behind the bush with her leg muscles aching, Keela was now not so sure.

Then Mali tapped her shoulder and pointed. Through the leaves Keela could see, small at first but getting bigger as it approached, a black bird floating through the sky. All of a sudden it cocked its head, tucked in its wings, and dropped down to land beside the coin.

Keela gasped.

The bird was magnificent. Blue-black feathers glistened in the sun. Its strong, curved beak gave it a proud look. Dark beady eyes darted left and right before the crow picked up the coin with its beak.

As it leapt into the air Mali and Keela hurried from their hiding place. The crow was already high in the sky by the time they took chase. The bird flew away from the castle, with Mali and Keela chasing as hard as they could below. Eventually the bird soared out of sight.

"Lost it," Keela panted, as Mali came to a halt beside her.

"At least we know which way it went," Mali said. "And it proves that Ruby is innocent, too."

But the king wasn't so easily convinced.

"This doesn't prove a bird took the necklace," the king said after Keela told him about the crow.

"We need to retrieve the necklace," Mali said afterwards. "That will prove it."

So the next day they went back to the spot where they had lost sight of the bird. They put another coin on the ground and hid behind a tree. Again, there was a long wait, but eventually the crow appeared. As it flew over it saw a glint from the shiny coin.

The crow dived and landed beside the coin. It looked around. It took the coin in its beak, then leapt into the air. And again Mali and Keela gave chase but again the bird disappeared from view.

"This isn't working," Keela said as they walked back to the castle. "We keep losing it."

So that afternoon they hatched another plan. The coin they placed for the crow the next day had a red ribbon attached to it with a blob of candle wax.

The coin was placed, shiny side up, where they had lost sight of the bird the day before. And, as expected, while they hid behind a bush, the crow swooped down and collected the coin. But this time, as it flew away, the red ribbon fluttered behind it.

"This way!" Mali called, chasing along behind.

After a few minutes, they stopped.

"Did you see which way?" Mali asked, his heart pounding.

"No," Keela answered. "It just vanished."

They scanned the sky. The crow was nowhere to be seen.

"Not again!" Mali said in frustration.

But then something colorful caught Keela's eye. Looking up, she spotted the red ribbon high in the branches of a tree. It was hanging over the side of a bird's nest.

"Mali – look!" she said, pointing. Standing beside the nest was the crow. It took to the air again, flying in the direction of the castle.

At the base of the tree Mali jumped, pulling himself up to the lowest branch. From there he climbed to the top of the tree as surely as if he were climbing a ladder. He walked along the branch, unconcerned about the height, until he reached the nest.

"Well?" Keela asked as Mali climbed down again.

Mali pulled a coin from his pocket. Then another, and then the third coin with the ribbon stuck to it. From his other pocket Mali pulled the queen's missing necklace. It sparkled in the sun.

Keela whooped with joy.

"There was something else in the nest too," Mali said. "Two little chicks!"

*

Keela and Ruby stood by the pond in the castle grounds, throwing crusts to the ducklings.

"Aren't you going to give them all of it?" Keela asked, noticing that Ruby still held a few slices of bread.

"I'm saving these for the crow," Ruby said.

"But the crow got you in trouble!" Keela said.

"Perhaps, but it has little mouths to feed too," Ruby replied. "And in some ways it did me a favor."

Keela looked at Ruby enquiringly.

"It helped me find out how much you care," Ruby said.

JUSTICE

Practicing justice is being fair. It is solving problems so everyone wins. You don't prejudge. You see people as individuals. You don't accept it when someone acts like a bully, cheats, or lies. Being a champion for justice takes courage. Sometimes when you stand for justice, you stand alone.

Keela didn't think it was fair that the maid was blamed for the missing necklace. She didn't believe the maid would steal so she stood up for her, working to solve the problem so that the maid could be proven innocent.

- *When you are aware of something that is unfair, is it easier to accept the injustice or to stand up against the injustice? Why?*
- *If someone is being bullied what are some of the ways you could practice justice?*
- *You notice something is missing from your room and you think your brother took it. How would you practice justice?*
- *Have you ever been in a situation that you felt was unjust? How did it feel? What would justice have looked like in that situation?*

LOYALTY

Loyalty is staying true to someone. It is standing up for something you believe in without wavering. It is being faithful to your family, country, school, friends, or ideals when the going gets tough as well as when things are good. With loyalty, you build relationships that last forever.

Keela is loyal to the maid – she doesn't believe what others are saying about her being a thief. Even though it is difficult to prove the maid's innocence, Keela stays loyal to her.

- *How do you think the maid felt when Keela demonstrated her loyalty toward her?*
- *Do you feel loyalty toward any things or people? Describe them.*
- *How could you show loyalty toward your friend when another group of children don't want to play with him or her?*
- *What does it feel like when a friend isn't loyal to you? What is the best thing about having a loyal friend?*
- *How would you show loyalty to yourself? What would that look like?*

CONFIDENCE

Confidence is having faith in someone. Self-confidence is trusting that you have what it takes to handle whatever happens. You feel sure of yourself and enjoy trying new things, without letting doubts or fears hold you back. When you have confidence in others, you rely on them.

Because he lives in a tree-house, Mali is a confident tree climber. He demonstrates confidence by climbing up to the bird's nest "as surely as if he were climbing a ladder". He trusts his abilities and feels sure of himself.

- *In what situations might it be helpful to call upon your self-confidence?*
- *When do you feel most confident? Least confident?*
- *How does a person with confidence go about trying something new or meeting new people?*
- *Where do you think confidence comes from?*
- *Who do you know who seems confident? What is it about them that makes you think they are confident?*

COMPASSION

Compassion is understanding and caring when someone is hurt or troubled, even if you don't know them. It is wanting to help, even if all you can do is listen and say kind words. You forgive mistakes. You are a friend when someone needs a friend.

Knowing that the crow has chicks in its nest, the maid saves bread so she can feed it. By caring and wanting to help she was demonstrating compassion.

- *How could you show compassion if someone in your class was feeling sad?*
- *Have you ever changed your mind about a person after you have imagined yourself in their shoes? What did that feel like?*
- *What are some things that you could do to help a new student at school feel more comfortable?*
- *What would compassion look like if you had a friend who was sick in the hospital?*
- *Have you ever felt compassion toward someone you didn't know? Toward an animal? What did you do?*

Flying with the Seagulls

Helpfulness ～ *Excellence* ～ *Courage* ～ *Joyfulness*

Mali smiled. The morning sun warmed his skin and the birds sang in the trees. It felt like a great day for an adventure!

I think I'll visit Keela today, he thought as he walked down the path towards his boat.

Keela watched Mali's boat draw closer and closer from her window in the top tower of the castle. She ran down to meet him on the pier.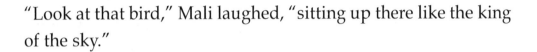

"Hi Mali!" she called as he arrived. "Great day isn't it?"

But before Mali could answer a seagull landed on the mast of his boat and let out a loud *SQUARK!*

"Look at that bird," Mali laughed, "sitting up there like the king of the sky."

The seagull leapt into the air and soared gracefully away.

"I wish I could fly like that," Keela sighed.

"Me too," Mali agreed. "Maybe we could if we had wings."

"Hey! Let's make some!" said Keela excitedly. "I'll get some sheets, and we can tie them to our arms. If we flap fast enough we might take off!"

On the lawn behind Keela's castle they ran around, flapping their wings as fast as they could, but their feet stayed firmly on the ground. They flapped and jumped. Nothing. They ran, flapped, leapt, and double-flapped. Still nothing.

"Mali, flying isn't as easy as I thought," Keela puffed. "I think we need to go and ask Lao. He always has an answer to a problem."

The waves sparkled before them as they sailed to Lao's island. They tied up the boat and walked the path to Lao's hut.

"So you want to be birds in the sky do you?" questioned wise old Lao. "First you must watch, then you will learn."

He pointed to a bird on the roof of his hut.

"Look," he said. "See the shape of his wings?"

As the bird stretched out its wings Mali noticed that they weren't just flat, but were rounded on top.

"To fly," Lao continued, "your wings will need to be like a bird's. The right shape, strong, and light!"

"And look there," the old man pointed high above them at a bird gliding overhead. "It's the air moving over his wings that keeps him up there. Come on, we have work to do!"

Lao used a stick to draw a picture in the dirt.

"We'll make bamboo frames like this," he explained, pointing at the picture. "I have some fabric that we can use to stretch over the top."

"But remember," Lao cautioned, "strong, light, and perfectly balanced. Take care to do it right and you might just fly!"

"This is great!" Mali said as he grabbed two pieces of bamboo to tie together.

While they worked, Keela looked over at Mali. He had quickly tied his frame together and was now pulling a sheet over it.

She looked over at Lao. He was taking his time to carefully measure each piece and was making sure his knots were tied tightly. Rather than rushing, Lao was checking and double-checking his work for balance and strength.

"Finished!" Mali announced when Keela and Lao were still only halfway through. He held up the wing proudly. It wobbled and flapped in the breeze.

Mali dozed in the sun while Lao and Keela finished making their wings.

Finally Lao announced, "I think we are ready."

Mali and Keela struggled to keep up with Lao as they carried their wings up a large sand dune. At the top a warm wind blew. The air coming in from the ocean was scooped upwards by the shape of the dune.

Lao pointed. "Watch," he said.

A seagull stood on the sand beside them. It stretched its wings, it leaned forward, and as the wind passed over its wings it lifted gracefully into the air.

"Now you," Lao nodded to Mali.

Mali picked up his wing and held it above his head. Taking a step forward he leaned in to the wind as he'd seen the bird do. The wind raced up the dune and in its blast the wing flapped loudly. The loose knots loosened further.

Creak... crack... CRUNCH!

"Oh no," groaned Mali, looking at the tangle of bamboo and fabric in his hands.

Lao put his hand on Mali's shoulder.

"Well, you could use my wing," Lao told him. "Or you could..."

"Make a new one," Mali picked up. "I'd really like to fly one I've made myself."

On the way back to the hut they discussed what went wrong and what was needed to fix it. They measured new lengths of bamboo carefully. Mali tied the knots as tight as he could. He checked his work, then checked again. It took a lot longer to build than the first one, but Mali was proud of the strong, well-balanced wing he carried back up the dune.

"Before we try out your new wing," Lao said to Mali. "Let's see how Keela's one flies."

Keela moved to the edge of the sand dune where the wind blew powerfully. She lifted her wing above her head. As the wind caught it Keela was surprised by its strength. It was both exciting and scary.

"Now lean forward," Lao shouted over the wind. "You'll be fine."

Keela felt as if she would tumble down the sand dune. She knew that even if she did, the worst that would happen would be a mouthful of sand. Even so, she felt nervous.

"I hope you're right, Lao," she said. She took a deep breath and leaned forward.

The blast of air passed over the wing and instead of falling down she was lifted up, above the sand dune.

"I'm flying!" Keela shouted with joy. She held on tight as she bobbed in the powerful wind. She ducked and dived and weaved.

Keela glowed with happiness as she landed on the sand.

"That was fantastic!" Keela said. "Mali, you'll LOVE it!"

Taking up his new wing, Mali moved to the edge of the dune.

The wind made his eyes water. In his hands the new wing felt strong. He leaned forward.

"Wowee!" Mali shouted as his feet left the ground. He was flying! He grinned as he was buffeted about.

"It's like sailing really fast in my boat!" he yelled above the wind. "Only better!"

He flew until his arms grew tired from holding on. It was time to let Lao have a turn.

To their surprise old Lao took a running jump and launched

himself off the dune into the warm evening air. He whooped with delight as the wind blew his beard up around his ears.

*

As the golden sun sank slowly into the ocean, Mali and Keela waved goodbye to their old friend and set sail for home.

That night, as he dropped into bed feeling tired but happy, Mali imagined he was floating on a puffy pillow of cloud pulled by six giant seagulls, and soon he was fast asleep.

HELPFULNESS

Helpfulness is being of service to others, doing thoughtful things that make a difference in their lives. Offer your help without waiting to be asked. Ask for help when you need it. When we help each other, we get more done. We make our lives easier.

———————————————— ⇒ ————————————————

When Princess Keela and Mali had tried everything they could think of to fly, Keela suggested they visit wise old Lao to ask for his help. Lao was known for his helpfulness and kindness. They knew he would help them if he could.

- *Do you know anyone who is always helpful?*
- *When you are being helpful how do you feel?*
- *Can you share a time that you needed help and you received it? Was it easy for you to ask for help? Why or why not?*
- *How could you be helpful if you notice that your friend looks sad?*
- *What could you do today to make someone else's life easier?*

EXCELLENCE

Excellence is doing your best, giving careful attention to every task and every relationship. Excellence is effort guided by a noble purpose. It is a desire for perfection. The perfection of a seed comes in the fruit. When you practice excellence, you bring your gifts to fruition. Excellence is the key to success.

———————————————— ⇒ ————————————————

Mali was in a hurry to make his wing. In his eagerness he didn't take care to ensure his wing was strong and well built. Keela was encouraged towards excellence by watching Lao work, who made sure he did a good job rather than a fast job.

- *Can you think of a time when you have worked hard towards excellence?*
- *If you got tired in the middle of an assignment or chore, what might excellence look like?*
- *How can you demonstrate excellence in your relationships with your friends or family?*
- *What are some of the things that you do with excellence? What do you consider your most excellent virtues?*
- *What difference does excellence make when we do something?*

COURAGE

Courage is bravery in the face of fear. You do the right thing even when it is hard or scary. When you are courageous, you don't give up. You try new things. You admit mistakes. Courage is the strength in your heart.

—————————————— ≈ ——————————————

The strong warm wind coming off the top of the sand dune was both exhilarating and scary for Keela. She needed to gather all her courage to overcome her nervousness.

- *I know you have displayed courage. How does it feel when you are courageous?*
- *Do you think performing for or playing in front of an audience requires courage? Why or why not?*
- *Doing something for the first time can be scary. What helps you to get past fear?*
- *Who have you seen display courage in performing their job?*
- *How could you display courage if you had broken your dad's favorite mug and no one else knew who did it?*

JOYFULNESS

Joyfulness is an inner sense of peace and happiness. You appreciate the gifts each day brings. Without joyfulness, when the fun stops, our happiness stops. Joy can carry us through the hard times even when we are feeling very sad. Joy gives us wings.

—————————————— ≈ ——————————————

Mali and Keela were filled with great joy at the success of the attempt to fly. Even though he is an old man, Lao also shows his joyfulness as he "whooped with delight as the wind blew his beard up around his ears".

- *What do you do that makes you feel joyful?*
- *Can you think of a person you know who shows a lot of joyfulness?*
- *Where do you think joy comes from?*
- *When you feel down or sad, what do you do to cheer yourself up?*
- *How could you be joyful doing a task that bores you?*

THE PUMPKIN AND THE FAIR

Diligence ⁓ Moderation ⁓ Flexibility ⁓ Modesty

"Noooo..." Mali shouted as he tried to catch the pumpkin.

CRACK!

Mali looked down at his prize pumpkin, shattered on the floor. He'd been looking out the window, to the field behind the castle where tables were being set up for the fair, and had accidentally bumped it off the kitchen bench.

"Oh dear," Keela said, placing a comforting hand on Mali's arm. "Now you can't enter the competition."

Mali had spent months growing that pumpkin. He'd prepared the soil carefully; he'd watered it regularly; he'd sung to it every day while tending to it. And it had grown and grown.

A real prize winner! Mali had thought to himself as he'd struggled to carry the pumpkin from his boat to the castle.

Keela clutched her stomach as it gave a loud rumble.

"And I've eaten so many plums I can't even think of making plum pie for the Best Pie Competition," she said.

That morning she had picked the juiciest plums she could reach in the royal orchard. There were more plums than she needed for the pie, so she ate one, then another, and *another...*

Mali and Keela had both desperately wanted to place an entry in the annual fair, due to start that very morning.

"Mali, I've made all this pastry, but..." Keela felt queasy just thinking about plum pie.

"Well, there's plenty of pumpkin here if you want to make pumpkin pie instead," Mali suggested.

"Mali, that's brilliant!" said Keela. "With a pumpkin this size we could make a huge pie!"

They did have a lot of pumpkin, but they didn't have much time. And there was another problem.

"There's no pie dish big enough to hold all this pumpkin," Keela said, looking through the kitchen cupboards.

They searched the kitchen for something big to use as a pie dish. Then Mali remembered the suit of armour that stood by the front door of the castle.

"There's a big shield with that suit of armour!" Mali said. "It's about the right size. We could use that as a pie dish!"

Mali fetched the shield. He scrubbed it clean while Keela chopped the pumpkin into small pieces and put them in a pot of hot water to cook. She added spices and sugar, then they rolled out the pastry. Once the pastry was laid over the shield they scooped the pumpkin in and covered it with another sheet of pastry. It was the biggest pie they had ever seen.

"We'd better pop it in the oven," Keela said, before stopping in her tracks.

"Oh no!" she said, clapping her hand to her forehead. "This is so big it won't fit in the oven!"

Mali looked at the oven and scratched his head. She was right. There was no way it would fit in.

Outside they could hear the crowds arriving for the fair. Entries for the pie competition were being called. Mali looked around desperately.

"There must be *something* we can bake this in," he said.

Keela's eyes lit up.

"The kiln!" she said. "The pottery kiln, out by the stables! It would fit in there."

With much puffing and panting they each took a side of the shield and carried the pie out to the kiln. Old Jim, the gardener, was removing a large clay pot from the kiln as they appeared.

"Is it still hot, Jim?" Keela asked.

Old Jim turned.

"Oh! 'Ullo, Princess." He said. Then his eyes settled on the huge pie. He took off his cap and scratched his head.

"It's hot enough to bake a pie, if that's what you mean," he added.

The three of them eased the pie carefully into the kiln, and then Keela raced to the fair. She ran to the pie competition table, dodging stilt-walkers and children with toffee apples.

"Hello, Keela," the head judge said, inspecting her list.

"I see your name is on here," she said, prodding the list. "But where is your pie?"

"It's still baking," Keela puffed, trying to catch her breath.

"Well, you had better get it here quickly," the head judge said. "We have to start the judging."

"I'll be back soon!" Keela called over her shoulder as she dashed away.

Back at the stables Old Jim opened the door of the kiln, and a great puff of smoke billowed out. They eased the pie out and placed it on a plank of wood. The pastry was golden brown. A smoky smell of roast pumpkin filled the air.

In the distance they heard an announcement.

"Entry to the pie competition closes in three minutes... last call for entries!"

Thanking Jim for his help, they lifted the plank and headed for the fair. People now crowded the field.

"Excuse me... coming through... sorry... pardon me..."

Keela and Mali were bumped and jostled as they looked for a way through. Mali tripped, and the pie slid dangerously close to the edge of the plank. It teetered, threatening to fall. But he found his footing and nudged the pie back into place.

"Two minutes until the pie competition closes."

People turned to see where the delicious smell was coming from. Eyes widened at the sight of the giant pie weaving through the crowd.

"One minute to go," came the announcement.

Through the crowd Keela could see the judging tables. The first table was laden with huge pumpkins. The next table was covered with delicious-looking cakes. And on the third were the pies, waiting to be judged.

As they passed the first table Keela let out a gasp.

"No!" she cried out.

Her dress had caught on the corner of the table and – *ripppp!* – it tore, right up the side! She scrambled to hold the fabric together and as she did so, she let go of the plank.

With all his strength, Mali held on, but the plank was now a ramp with the pie sliding down it. He steered the sliding pie towards the pie competition table.

The judge's eyes widened as the huge pie flew through the air towards them. It slid across the table, and came to a stop before the head judge.

"Are we in time?" Keela asked desperately.

"Y-y-yes..." the head judge stammered.

Mali wiped his brow in relief, and Keela flopped to the ground, exhausted.

Later, a crowd gathered as the head judge stood to announce the results. Third prize was announced, and then second.

The crowd hushed with anticipation as the winning pie was announced.

"The winning pie this year was a very unusual entry," the head judge said to the waiting crowd. "It was chosen for its distinctive flavour – pumpkin, with a lovely wood-smoke taste. The winner is Princess Keela!"

The crowd clapped. Keela moved to stand, but, feeling her torn dress flap around her legs, she thought again.

"Mali, would you mind," she nodded to where the head judge held out the winner's ribbon.

"The prize belongs to you anyway," Keela said to Mali when he returned. "You grew the beautiful pumpkin inside the pie."

At the castle Keela changed while Mali cut the pie into slices to share around.

"Have a slice," he said, handing Keela a large piece when she returned.

Keela's stomach gurgled, reminding her of all the plums she'd gobbled earlier.

"Maybe just that small one," Keela said, pointing to a thin slice.

"I don't want to overdo it... *again!*" she said, laughing.

DILIGENCE

Diligence is working hard and doing your absolute best. You take special care by doing things step by step. Diligence helps you to get things done with excellence and enthusiasm. Diligence leads to success.

⤜

Mali was keen to grow a champion pumpkin. With diligence he'd carefully prepared the soil, and then spent months tending to his pumpkin; watering it and caring for it every day.

- *How might you practice diligence if you were training a puppy? Or writing "Thank You" cards after your birthday party?*
- *Does paying attention to what you are doing help in practicing diligence? How or how not?*
- *What would diligence look like if you had a difficult task to do and you wanted to give up in the middle of it?*
- *What might your room look like if you didn't clean it up with diligence? What would it look like if you did use diligence?*
- *Name some professions that require diligence. What might happen if builders did a careless job of building a skyscraper? Doctors in performing surgery?*

MODERATION

Moderation is creating a healthy balance in your life between work and play, rest and exercise. You don't overdo or get swept away by the things you like. You use your self-discipline to take charge of your life and your time.

⤜

Keela ate so many plums before the fair that she felt too sick to make a plum pie. She showed a lack of moderation by eating too many. In the end she showed moderation by choosing a smaller piece so that she didn't overdo it again.

- *It can be easy to get swept away with the things we like. Can you think of some things that would be unhealthy if we did them too much?*
- *What would moderation look like if you have a habit of staying up late at night reading or playing and then feel too sleepy to get up in the morning?*
- *Are there any areas in your life where you could create more balance? In what areas could you spend more time or less time to create more balance?*
- *Name some things that people can overdo or become addicted to if they don't practice moderation.*

FLEXIBILITY

Flexibility is being open to change. You consider others' ideas and feelings and don't insist on your own way. Flexibility gives you creative new ways to get things done. You get rid of bad habits and learn new ones. Flexibility helps you to keep changing for the better.

───────────────────────── ⁀ ─────────────────────────

Mali had planned to enter the Biggest Pumpkin Competition. Keela had planned to make a plum pie for the Best Pie Competition. By being open to change they allowed the creativity of their new plan to lead them to a result they hadn't even considered earlier.

- *Can you think of a time when you have been flexible with your plans or ideas?*
- *What would flexibility look like if your family had a fun picnic planned that had to be cancelled because of bad weather?*
- *How could you show flexibility if you were building a tower of blocks that keeps falling down before it is very high?*
- *What would flexibility look like if your sister was visiting a friend overnight and it is her job to wash the dishes?*

MODESTY

Modesty is having self-respect. When you value yourself with quiet pride, you accept praise with humility and gratitude. Modesty is being comfortable with yourself and setting healthy boundaries about your body and your privacy.

───────────────────────── ⁀ ─────────────────────────

Keela didn't want to stand in front of the crowd to collect her winner's ribbon with her dress ripped up the side. She was practicing modesty by keeping her body private. She was also being modest by saying to Mali that the winner's ribbon really belonged to him.

- *This story shows modesty in two ways (Keela's privacy, and Keela accepting praise with humility). Did you notice that both examples demonstrate her quiet pride and self-respect?*
- *How might you enjoy an accomplishment or victory and still be modest about it?*
- *How do you use self-respect in choosing what clothes you will wear?*
- *How would it feel to be on a team that won an important game and one person on the team takes all the credit for the win?*
- *What would you do or say if you felt like someone was touching your body inappropriately?*

SMOKE ON THE HORIZON
Thankfulness ～ *Responsibility* ～ *Courtesy* ～ *Purposefulness*

𝓜ali squinted through the telescope.

"Look lower, on the horizon," Lao told him. "It looks like a dark cloud, but it's smoke."

"From a volcano?" Keela asked.

Lao nodded.

"I've been watching it for weeks," he said, "and every day it's been getting darker – thicker with ash."

Later that day, Mali and Keela sat on the jetty in front of the castle. Across the water was Mali's island, with its trees lush and green in the afternoon sun.

"We're lucky aren't we?" Mali commented. "Imagine living near a volcano about to blow its top."

Keela closed her eyes and imagined the trees and beaches covered in poisonous ash and burning lava. She shivered.

Her eyes opened suddenly. "Suppose there are people living where that volcano is! Mali, they might need to be rescued."

"That's true," Mali nodded. "But Lao said it's likely to erupt any day. It's too far away for my boat to get there in time – we'd need a faster boat."

"My father has a ship," Keela said, getting to her feet. "And it's fast."

But when they asked, the king shook his head.

"The captain is away so there's nobody to skipper it," he told them.

"Mali could do it!" Keela said.

The king laughed.

"It's a sailing ship, not a little boat," he chuckled. "It takes a lot of skill to captain something like that."

"With respect, sir," Mali said. "I've been sailing my whole life. I can do it."

They talked it through, and the more they talked, the more convinced the king became that they should attempt to get to the volcano.

"You're right," the king said. "There may be people in danger. We should try to help if we can, but time is against us, so let's move quickly."

They worked through the night, planning and preparing. They grew weary as the hours drew on, but the thought of people stranded on a fearsome volcano drove them to keep going.

By morning the ship was ready for the task ahead.

And as the sun rose, the king's ship sailed out to sea, with Mali at the helm.

They picked up Bongo from Mali's island, and then, passing old Lao's island, they collected him too, before steering the mighty ship towards the smoke on the horizon.

"It's an impressive ship," Mali said, grinning, as Keela came to stand with him. "And an impressive crew too."

He nodded towards the king and queen chatting on the deck

with Lao. Keela smiled at Bongo, swinging happily from the ropes high up the main mast.

As they sailed, the sea became rougher. Waves slammed into the side of the vessel. It took all of Mali's strength to hold the ship on course.

"We're getting closer," Keela shouted above the roar of the wind.

Ahead the volcano was now visible, towering over the small island it stood on.

The air was thick with foul-smelling smoke. Lava oozed in hot red flows down the side of the volcano.

"I'll take us in as close as I can," Mali shouted.

Nearer the shore, the waves were smaller. But here currents swirled – dragging and pulling at the ship. Mali's blistered hands gripped the wheel as he fought to avoid rocks that jutted through the waves.

They circled the island, searching for inhabitants. There were no huts, no tracks – no sign of people.

The volcano was now throwing flaming rocks into the sky. They crashed, hissing and steaming, into the ocean.

"It's going to blow!" Lao shouted. "We need to get out of here."

Suddenly Keela pointed to the shore.

"Look!" she yelled.

Two great streams of lava flowed into the sea. Huddled between the fiery flows was a troop of frightened monkeys.

"I can't get the ship any closer without beaching her," said Mali. "The only way to reach them is by rowboat. I'll go if someone can hold the ship steady."

"I'll hold it here, but be quick Mali," the king urged as a ball of flaming lava hissed into the ocean beside them.

Lao, Keela and the queen lowered the rowboat from the stern of the ship. As soon as it touched the water, Mali pulled hard on the oars. In front Bongo held on tightly.

After the sturdy ship, the little rowboat felt fragile. They were tossed about as they rowed between rocks.

"Just about there," Mali assured Bongo, as the water bubbled and boiled around them.

With a wave behind them, they surfed the boat on to the beach. Bongo leapt to the sand and ran to the monkeys.

Between the streams of lava, the air was hot and thick with smoke. The monkeys huddled together, wide-eyed with fear. However, with Bongo encouraging and urging, they followed him.

Together, Mali and Bongo helped the scared monkeys on to the rowboat.

"Quick, Bongo!" Mali called as the lava streams joined in the middle to form one huge fiery flow, bearing down on them swiftly.

Mali pushed off. He heaved with all his might on the oars and the monkey-laden boat groaned through the waves, away from the steaming shore.

With aching arms, Mali finally drew the rowboat alongside the ship.

"Well done," Lao said as he helped Mali aboard.

The volcano rumbled and shook.

"Let's go!" the king called as he pulled on the wheel. The ship turned. Wind filled the sails and a sizzling wake trailed behind the fleeing ship.

Looking back, the crew watched in awe as the volcano erupted in a blaze of fireworks against the inky blue sky.

At the helm Lao and Mali navigated by the stars as they sailed through the night towards home.

Hours later, as the morning sun glowed on the horizon, they arrived back at Lao's island.

"Are you sure about the monkeys living here with you?" Mali asked Lao.

"It's perfect for them," Lao answered. "It's safe, there's plenty of food, and I can look after them until they've settled in. They'll love it here!"

Lao stood on the beach with the rescued monkeys and waved goodbye.

On deck the tired crew waved back.

Standing with the king and queen, Keela could hardly keep her eyes open.

"Thank you for helping," she said, as the king placed his arm around her shoulder.

Above them, in the ropes, Bongo swung upside down. He waved down to Mali, who grinned and waved back.

"We're home," the queen said as the castle came into view.

Across the water from the castle Mali's island was green and welcoming in the morning sun.

"Home," Mali said. "It's good to be home."

THANKFULNESS

Thankfulness is being grateful for what we have. It is an attitude of gratitude for learning, loving and being. Appreciate the little things that happen around you and within you every day. Think positively. Thankfulness brings contentment.

———————————— ⌁ ————————————

Mali and Keela thought about the damage an erupting volcano could do and realized how lucky they were to live in a beautiful, safe place. They were thankful for what they have.

• *Can you name some things that you are grateful for? How do you show your thankfulness for these things?*
• *What are some things that you appreciate about yourself?*
• *Who are people in your life that you are grateful for? What is it about them that you appreciate?*
• *When do you find it most difficult to be grateful? What could you do to help yourself be thankful?*

RESPONSIBILITY

Being responsible means others can trust you to do things with excellence. You accept accountability for your actions. When you make a mistake, you offer amends instead of excuses. Responsibility is the ability to respond ably and to make smart choices.

———————————— ⌁ ————————————

The king entrusted Mali with the task of sailing the royal ship to the volcanic island. It was difficult sailing through the rough seas but Mali took his responsibility seriously – first by ensuring they got to the volcano quickly, and then by courageously saving the monkeys.

• *What are some responsibilities that you have now that you didn't have when you were younger?*
• *What would responsibility look like if you promised to do a chore, but watched a TV program instead?*
• *Responsible people learn from a mistake and fix it without getting defensive. Describe a time when you observed someone who acted this way.*
• *Name a time when you acted responsibly and describe how you felt. Name a time when you didn't act responsibly and describe how that felt.*

COURTESY

Courtesy is being polite and having good manners. When you speak and act courteously, you give others a feeling of being valued and respected. Greet people pleasantly. Bring courtesy home. Your family needs it most of all. Courtesy helps life to go smoothly.

When speaking with the king about the need to find a fast vessel to attempt the rescue, Mali spoke with courtesy. Even though she was exhausted, Keela remembered to thank her father for helping.

- *What are some courtesy words or expressions that you use?*
- *Do you think people react differently to you when you are courteous rather than when you are not courteous? Describe how they might react.*
- *What is the difference between requesting a favor from someone and demanding it? What words are used for requesting? What words are used for demanding?*
- *What words might you say to someone if you realized that you had forgotten to be courteous to them?*

PURPOSEFULNESS

Being purposeful is having a clear focus. Begin with a vision for what you want to accomplish, and concentrate on your goals. Do one thing at a time, without scattering your energies. Some people let things happen. When you are purposeful, you make things happen.

Once they had decided to attempt to help the inhabitants of the volcanic island, they worked with purposefulness throughout the night to prepare the ship. They focused their energies on achieving their goal.

- *Describe a time when you had a clear idea of something that you wanted to do or accomplish. How did you go about it? Were you successful?*
- *Name a successful person and describe how you think they practiced purposefulness.*
- *What would purposefulness look like if you found yourself daydreaming while doing your schoolwork?*
- *When do you find it most difficult to stay focused? What could you do to make it easier?*

Index of Virtues

About The Virtues Project™

The Virtues Project™ is a global project offering personal, professional and community development programs and materials to help people of all cultures live by their highest values.

It was founded in 1991 by Linda Kavelin-Popov, Dr. Dan Popov, and John Kavelin, to provide strategies to inspire the practice of virtues in everyday life.

Researching the world's diverse sacred traditions, they discovered more than 360 virtues at the heart of all beliefs about the meaning and purpose of life. They discovered that at the heart of all spiritual traditions are virtues, described as the essence of the human spirit and the content of our character.

A guide containing fifty-two of these universal virtues was published to help parents bring out the best in their children and in themselves. Strategies were developed to restore the practice of virtues in everyday life. Books and support materials followed as word of The Virtues Project™ spread.

The Virtues Project™ materials are being applied in families, schools, prisons, corporations, social-service programs, child-care centers, indigenous communities, and diverse faith communities throughout the world.

The Virtues Project™ provides life-skill strategies that help individuals to live more reverent, purposeful lives, supports parents to raise children of strong moral character, inspires excellence, commitment and service in the workplace, and helps schools and communities to build a climate of safety and caring.

During the International Year of the Family, the United Nations Secretariat and World Conference of Cities and Corporations honored The Virtues Project™ as "a model global program for families of all cultures".

The Virtues Project™ is not about the practices or beliefs of any one religion. It is sourced in the teachings about virtues found in the sacred traditions of all cultures. Its purpose is to support all people, both those who are religious and those who are not, to awaken the virtues of their character.

Why virtues? Why not values?... Virtues are simpler than values. Virtues are the qualities of our character. Values are whatever we consider important. We can value anything from money and power to the Golden Rule. Values are culture-specific, while virtues, such as courage, honor, justice, and love, are the common elements of character and spirituality universally valued by all cultures.

The Adventures of Mali & Keela uses the fifty-two virtues found in *The Virtues Project Educator's Guide*. Designed primarily for counselors, teachers, caregivers, and youth leaders, this is a guide to creating cultures of caring and integrity in our schools, day care centers, and youth programs.

See **www.virtuesproject.com** for more information.

About the Author

Jonathan Collins lives with his wife and two children on an island in the South Pacific. It's not quite as small as Mali's island, although it is equally as beautiful... it is the South Island of New Zealand. When not writing, Jonathan works as a creative director and communications manager. This is his fifth children's book.

Acknowledgements

I am extremely thankful for the generosity of so many people who have helped to bring this book to reality. Natalie Collins for her endless support and love, and Liam and Jemma Collins – the inspiration for Mali and Keela – for patience and understanding while Dad disappeared to the computer for so many hours. At Personhood Press, Cathy and Bradley Winch have been a pleasure to work with, thank you for your trust, your hard work, for everything. Unsung hero of the book is editor and mentor, Sean O'Connor, whose guiding hand and keen eye have been invaluable. Enormous thanks go to my writing buddy, Janice Healey, who worked with commitment and enthusiasm to get Mali's adventures down on paper – your helpfulness and creativity is very much appreciated. Many thanks also to Jenny Cooper, whose charming illustrations have brought these stories to life.

I give thanks also to Linda Popov, who encouraged me to write The Adventures of Mali & Keela, *and for creating* The Virtues Project™ *in the first place. Her work has had a profoundly positive impact on so many people. Thanks also to PRO-ED for granting permission for excerpts from* The Virtues Project™ Educator's Guide *to be included in this book.*

Jonathan Collins